"Thank you, Marcus. I would love to come to Fiji with you."

A cautious grin spread across Marcus's face.

"Lucy, I want you to know this is purely professional."

"Of course. I mean, of course, I didn't..." She was stuttering and stammering like someone who had obviously considered the propriety and possibilities of two people who were pretty obviously attracted to one another spending a weekend in tropical, romantic surroundings...

"Lucy, I didn't mean to make you uncomfortable or make things difficult for you. This is purely professional."

"I know."

"Lucy, I know it's none of my business, and you can tell me to butt out, but do you have a partner? Are you seeing anyone? Someone who might not..."

"No. That is, no, I'm not seeing anyone. I'm single."

Someone or something seemed to suck the air from the room. Marcus froze. Lucy held her breath. That was what he thought she was worried about? That she had a boyfriend who might not like that she was going to tropical Fiji for a few days with her gorgeous boss?

Dear Reader,

Have you ever had to keep a secret? Have you ever had to keep a secret from your boss?

Since having a baby when she was a teenager, Lucy has had a lot to deal with. So she's relieved to have finally finished studying and won the job of her dreams, but consciously or not, she doesn't tell her sexy new boss about her son. As the weeks go on and their attraction grows, it becomes harder to keep her secret. But the closer she grows to Marcus, the harder it is to tell him.

Marcus lives for his work. When tragedy tore his family apart, he resolved never to love or have a family of his own again. But there's something different about Lucy. She's more mature than any of his other employees, and it's driving him out of his mind that he can't figure out why that is...

I hope you all enjoy reading Lucy and Marcus's story.

Justine xx

Fiji Escape with Her Boss

Justine Lewis

Recycling programs
for this product may
not exist in your area.

ISBN-13: 978-1-335-73710-6

Fiji Escape with Her Boss

Copyright © 2023 by Justine Lewis

For questions and comments about the quality of this book,
please contact us at CustomerService@Harlequin.com.

Harlequin Enterprises ULC
22 Adelaide St. West, 41st Floor
Toronto, Ontario M5H 4E3, Canada
www.Harlequin.com

Printed in U.S.A.

Justine Lewis writes uplifting, heartwarming contemporary romances. She lives in Australia with her hero husband, two teenagers and outgoing puppy. When she isn't writing, she loves to walk her dog in the bush near her house, attempt to keep her garden alive and search for the perfect frock. She loves hearing from readers and you can visit her at justinelewis.com.

Books by Justine Lewis

Harlequin Romance

Billionaire's Snowbound Marriage Reunion

Visit the Author Profile page
at Harlequin.com.

For Tricia, who never let me give up.

CHAPTER ONE

THIS WAS AWKWARD.

Any sensible thoughts Lucy Spencer might have had ten seconds ago deserted her like an unfaithful boyfriend. A gentle but persistent thrum pulsed in her throat as Marcus Hawke showed her into the largest office she'd ever had the pleasure of stepping into. The view over the lush greenery of the Botanic Garden stretched to the sparkling waters of Sydney Harbour and took the last of her breath away. The carpet was so thick her new shoes sank into it, and the brown leather of the armchair Marcus motioned for her to sit in was the softest her backside had the pleasure of sitting on. But Lucy barely registered any of those things.

Her thoughts scrambled for the responses she had preprepared to the interview questions. Responses she had been rehearsing in her head for *days*.

All gone.

Forgotten with one look at the man who was interviewing her.

This was her dream job, the one she'd been studying towards for four long, difficult years. Oracle Creative was the most successful new creative agency in Sydney. Its founder, the man standing in front of her now, was the most brilliantly original advertising executive to emerge on the scene in years. She had studied some of his campaigns as part of her university courses.

Lucy had seen Marcus's high-resolution profile picture on the agency's website. In that black-and-white photo he was looking directly at the camera, his eyes challenging, his lips not exactly smiling, but not frowning either. Daring you to disagree with him. He was undoubtedly handsome. Dark hair, clipped short, with perfectly proportioned, symmetrical features. He looked benignly handsome in two dimensions and two tones. But in three dimensions and full colour, lit by the morning sun with the type of lighting perfection that would make Annie Leibovitz weep, he was unsurpassable. The living, breathing, moving version of him was a sight to behold. His long, lean limbs moved with the strength and nonchalance of a big cat. His posture was humbling, so she sat straighter. His eyes were incisive, so she paid attention. His skin glowed and her cheeks felt hot. And when he spoke, his deep voice vibrated in her belly.

Nothing in her life—and at twenty-three years of age, she'd already been through a lot—had quite prepared her for the physical reaction she was having right now to this man.

It was the most important moment in her fledgling career and she was struggling to breathe.

Panting like an overeager puppy, not the sophisticated, accomplished designer she was attempting to be.

Awkward.

Autopilot seemed to take over and she must have managed to answer some questions because Marcus kept firing more at her and nodding, even smiling, as she answered. Instead of giving her confidence, his smiling made things worse. When he smiled, her insides melted. She felt vibrations in parts of her that hadn't stirred in years. Somehow, she had no idea how, she managed to tell him about her degree, majoring in graphic design and communications. She told him about the experience she had gained in her casual position at a boutique graphic design firm. He asked her what piece of work she was most proud of and which designers she admired. Thank goodness she'd been practicing with her mother every night after Lachie went to bed. There was a lot to be said for rote learning, though she knew that when her mother asked later that evening what questions Marcus had asked her, she wouldn't be able to tell her.

'Do you have any questions for me?' he asked.

This question, however, brought her mind crashing back into her body. And her body firmly back to the reality of her life. She had prepared several questions she wanted to ask a potential employer. *Can you tell me about the flexible work arrangements? Your carer's leave policy? Is it possible to purchase leave to cover the school holidays?*

Instead she asked him what the company's culture was like. Safe.

She knew, legally, she didn't have to tell him about Lachie. She knew, *legally*, he couldn't refuse to hire her if he knew she was a single mother.

'We're a young office, dynamic. Dedicated. I won't lie to you; I expect my employees to work hard. I work hard. I haven't taken a day off in years. The job is….' Marcus rubbed his jaw with a powerful hand and studied her before adding, 'It's my whole life.'

Lucy nodded.

He's telling you you're going to have to give the job everything. Yeah, and he's also telling you that he's single.

Marcus continued. 'The job will involve long hours but you would be well remunerated. And you would have the opportunity to work on some of the most exciting campaigns in the country. Would any of that be a problem for you?'

He leaned forward, only slightly, but still enough that the hairs on the back of her neck noticed and stood to attention.

She wanted this job so much. More than almost anything.

And sitting there, in the spectacular office,

with the city at her feet and the most handsome man she'd ever seen sitting on a sofa across from her, smiling, waiting for her to speak, felt like some sort of reward. Karma. *Finally* something was going right in her life. Finally *she* was the winner. Finally she had done something right.

She shook her head. 'It wouldn't be a problem at all.'

'And this is you.' Tara, Oracle Creative's young office manager, pointed to a large white desk, empty apart from the twenty-eight-inch computer monitor. Lucy's heart almost stopped at the sight of the state-of-the-art computer. Every designer's dream.

'Thank you,' Lucy said as she placed her oversized and overworn handbag on the pristine desk.

'The notebooks and pens are for you too.' A selection of notebooks in all sizes and colours and several packets of coloured pens and pencils were stacked neatly in one corner of the desk. 'I have a stationery addiction. The cupboard's over there so help yourself to anything else you need. I love ordering more.' Tara grinned.

Lucy warmed to Tara instantly, though she was unused to someone bending this far backwards to help her. The whole thing—being here, having Tara being so friendly and helpful—was like a dream.

'Login details are here.' Tara handed Lucy a

bright pink Post-it note. 'If you have any problems logging in, just let me know. In fact, if you need any help at all, just yell. Well, maybe don't yell. My office is just over there.' She pointed over the other cubicles and down to the end of the corridor.

Lucy nodded. There was so much to get her head around.

The foyer and corridors of the offices were lined with large, framed photos of the agency's most successful campaigns, but in the nonpublic areas it was different. The office, as far as she could tell from the brief tour Tara had given her, was a mix of conventional desks and cubicles and unconventional breakout areas with couches, long tables as well as half-hidden nooks and booths for quieter conversations. Bright green plants created calming barriers between work areas. Lucy's desk was white, but her chair was yellow. She looked around the neighbouring cubicles. Their walls were covered with sketches, prints and photos.

She glanced down and spied the framed photo of Lachie in her handbag. He was wearing a Superman suit and sitting at the top of the slide at their local park, smiling like he thought he was about to fly. Lucy looked around at the other desks. Everyone had photos stuck to their partitions but they were of friends, wild nights out. Parties. No kids. Absolutely no babies.

She would bide her time. She'd have to tell them about Lachie eventually, even though, she realised, no one expected a twenty-three-year-old recent graduate to be a mother. She knew she looked young. She always had. Especially at seventeen and still now. With light brown hair, cheeks that stubbornly refused to shift from baby-faced to bombshell, she hardly looked like a sophisticated woman of the world. Her youthful appearance had attracted her more attention than she may have otherwise received as a teenage mother.

'Is he your younger brother?' was a common remark. If she felt strong, or if it was someone who needed to know her business, she would set them straight.

But if they were just a nosy stranger prying into her business, she would just nod. It was easier than seeing the look on their faces.

This wouldn't be the first time she'd lied.

Not that she was planning on lying, exactly. Just maybe not volunteering the truth *immediately.*

Lucy logged on to the computer system with remarkably little pain and started exploring Oracle's intranet site. She hadn't been allocated a project yet. When he'd called to offer her the job, Marcus had indicated there would be some exciting new projects coming up, though he wasn't at liberty to tell her exactly what they were. In any event, he said there were lots of opportunities for a designer with her qualifications.

Oracle Creative, or OC, as she'd heard Marcus refer to it, was the fastest growing agency in Sydney, though it still wasn't as big as the more established firms. Around thirty people all up. She would report to the head of the design team and Marcus Hawke himself.

Tara walked down the central corridor and said loudly enough for everyone to hear, 'Meeting with Marcus in the boardroom starting in two minutes.'

'What?' Lucy looked up. She wasn't prepared for a meeting. She wasn't prepared for anything at all.

'Just went in the calendar. Likes to keep us on our toes.'

Great. Though, if the last five years had taught her anything, it was how to handle last-minute changes of plans. She grabbed one of the notebooks and pens Tara had left for her and followed the others into the boardroom.

Like Marcus's office, the boardroom faced east over the glistening harbour. Her fellow employees took seats around the long table. Lucy chose one that left her back to the view, as she didn't need further distractions. Not today.

The chief distraction she was determined to block out entered the room shortly afterwards. Everyone in the room fell silent as he strode through the doorway that suddenly seemed smaller. He was the boss after all, but the effect he had on time and space reminded her of *Alice in Wonderland*. A room that was once spacious, was now small and tight. A clock hand that once ticked at the traditional pace, now moved in slow motion. Lucy's pulse, which had once moved at the same rate of the clock hand, now raced. Marcus wore a dark blue business shirt, no tie, top button open—so help her, she could just make out the soft skin of his collarbone. She closed her eyes and inhaled a deep, steadying breath. His business pants were slim fit, flattering like all get out. But she suspected that Marcus would look better the less he was wearing.

She pushed the thought away. She felt the heat rising in her cheeks even before his staggeringly blue eyes met hers and he nodded. She smiled and nodded back. She both hoped and feared she'd be working closely with Marcus. Though it probably would have been better for her sanity to be working more closely with Daphne, head of design. Daphne was certainly gorgeous, but Daphne did not send Lucy's pulse into levels that would shatter a blood pressure monitor.

Instead of her handsome boss, Lucy tried to concentrate on her new colleagues. See if she could match the names Tara had quickly rattled off as they had walked down the corridor to the correct faces. Despite her best efforts, she was having trouble dragging her eyes from Marcus, who now commanded the attention of the room.

'Thanks, everyone,' he said as the last of the people entered and found vacant seats. 'I've asked you all in here today to let you know that we've been invited by OZ Airways to pitch a new campaign to promote the airline. We all know that travel and tourism is suffering at the moment the world over. The industry is in crisis. The brief is simple—a full media campaign to restore confidence to travel and the airline's reputation. So no biggie.'

Giggles tittered around the room. Marcus's face broke into a wide grin. His eyes sparkled and the effect was dazzling. Like the sun reflecting off the water in the harbour.

'If we win this, it will be easily the biggest account Oracle has run. It would secure our place as one of Australia's elite agencies. It would make us one of the most influential.'

Something caught in his voice as he spoke those last words. She glanced around to see how the others reacted, but their faces remained impassive.

'We're working to a tight time frame. We have to present a provisional pitch to the advertising director at OZ within three weeks.'

Lucy was new to the whole business, but that did seem very tight.

'And if they like our provisional pitch, we'll be invited to present a full presentation to their board. At Oracle, we're a team. This is such a huge opportunity for the firm I want to use every ability and idea you all have. I don't just want to hear from the creatives, but all of you. With any ideas. I thought we would start with a brainstorming session. Let's go around the table. One idea each. There are no wrong ideas. What do you think of when someone says, "Airline travel"?'

Was he serious? She was a designer, not a copywriter. And this was her first day. She hadn't even had a cup of tea yet.

Marcus pointed to the young man immediately to his left. 'Go.'

'Cramped seats.'

'Bad food.'

'Long queues.'

Laughter.

'Backpacking around Europe,' a woman with two nose piercings said.

Marcus nodded. The mood shifted.

'Exotic destinations.'

'Tropical islands.'

'Bar hopping in NYC.'

The words were moving quickly around the table like a Mexican wave and she had to get ready to jump. What did she think of when she heard the words 'Airline travel'?

She thought of the one and only time she'd taken Lachie on a plane to Brisbane and he'd cried the whole way. She thought of how relieved she'd been to get home again. She thought of how

Lachie's father, Alex, had been overseas for holidays twice since Lachie had been born. She thought of her school friends having gap years. Things she'd missed out on.

'Coming home,' she blurted. She knew it was the wrong answer, but it was all she could think of. 'I'm sorry,' she added quickly. 'I'm not thinking like a tourist.'

Her garbled apology drew Marcus's eyes away from the others and to her. 'Lucy,' he said. 'Has everyone met Lucy?' Most people around the table smiled, but shook their heads. 'She's a designer, joined the creative team this morning.'

'About half an hour ago,' Lucy added, to explain her complete lack of having a clue.

'Coming home. No, I like it,' Marcus said and gave her a smile that scorched her cheeks. 'Coming home safely is as important as leaving. And welcoming people to our home is equally important.'

A hum of agreement buzzed around the room.

Marcus bent down and typed something into his tablet.

This was her first professional job. She had so many worries about how it would all work that she couldn't even begin to list them. She'd thought that getting into the city on time after dropping Lachie at school and getting back in time to pick him up from after-school care was going to be her biggest concern. Finding the energy to look after him, while also working full-time, was another. Fitting in at work, doing a good job. These were things she'd worried about.

But figuring out how to ensure her core temperature didn't rise five degrees every time she looked at her new boss had not been in the top five. It hadn't even been on the list.

Marcus moved smoothly around the table to where she sat. When he was a metre away, she felt the air in the room shift completely shift, like a gentle wind had passed through. He looked down at her with his blue eyes. Aquamarine. Azure. Turquoise. All on the blue-green side of the colour wheel. Like a tropical lagoon. Did he have this effect on everyone? How did anyone get anything done around here?

'And?' He was staring at her, like he was waiting for a response, but she hadn't heard the question. Too busy deciding what shade of blue Marcus's eyes were.

The plan was to be cool, calm and sophisticated. Like she had lived her life to plan, like there was nothing out of the ordinary about her at all. So much for that plan.

'Tell us all a bit about yourself,' he said.

Everyone was looking at her. Assessing her. They were all young, like her, but dressed sharper. Their hair no more than three weeks out from a cut and colour. Many of them had facial piercings. Most of them had tattoos.

She had her natural hair colour. Her skin was resolutely tattoo free. Her only scars were the not insignificant scars of motherhood. She didn't even have her ears pierced for crying out loud. She was about as hip as your average eighty-year-old. And now her face was the colour of a tomato and they'd all see how unsophisticated and deeply uncool she was.

'I'm Lucy Spencer. I've just graduated from Northern Sydney University. I've also done some work for a small agency in North Sydney and I'm really excited about the opportunity to work at Oracle.'

There, that was the sort of thing he meant, wasn't it?

Not only was this her dream job, but it was almost definitely her only shot at an agency as prestigious as Oracle. This job would finally allow her and Lachie to move out of her parents' house. She loved her parents and they adored Lachie. They insisted she could stay forever, but that had never been part of Lucy's plan. She couldn't let them support her indefinitely. She couldn't expect anyone else to take responsibility for her life choices.

Marcus nodded and then finally his searing gaze was on the woman to Lucy's left and her skin began to cool.

'Let's start again. The first word you think of when I say, "Airline travel."'

'Cancelled plans.'

A collective groan went up.

Marcus shook his head. 'I told you, there are no wrong answers.'

'Business lounges.'

'First class seats.'

'Asia.'

'Jet lag.'

They went around the table a few more times as Marcus silently assessed them. Occasionally he typed something into his tablet.

Eventually he nodded. 'Thanks everyone. Daphne, Liam and...' His blue eyes scanned the room. 'And Lucy. Please stay. You will be the core team to begin with. No doubt there will be opportunities for the rest of you to get involved at some stage, but for now, you can get back to what you were doing.'

When the others had left, Liam and Daphne picked up their things and moved around the table, closer to Marcus. Lucy reluctantly followed.

'Congratulations, dream team,' Marcus began. 'I won't lie and tell you this'll be easy, but hopefully it will be a career highlight. And if we win, a headline for your resume. But this is going to consume you for the next month. For the next six weeks you will live and breathe OZ Airways. Why should people travel? What will be they be missing out on if they don't? Every country in the world is fighting for the tourist dollar at the moment. Why would someone want to choose Australia and OZ Airways above anyone else?'

She *should* be happy; it was her first morning in this job and she'd already been asked to work on Oracle's biggest project. A normal person would be chuffed. An ordinary person wouldn't have doubt churning in their stomach.

'Let's meet back here at three. Bring big ideas and lots of enthusiasm.'

Marcus's eyes focused tightly on Lucy. 'There are no wrong answers.'

Lucy stood, not quite breathing, desperate to get out of the meeting room and take a big deep breath of air that wasn't the same air that Marcus had been breathing for the past half hour.

Not that she could relax.

Back at her desk, she finally met the occupant of the workstation next to hers. The woman was also in her midtwenties. Her short dark hair cut into a sharp style. The kind of haircut you got if you were not just stylish but brave as well.

'Hi, I'm Amy and this is Janelle,' the woman said.

'Where have you come from?' Janelle asked.

'I just finished university.'

'Oh. You've got a degree?' Amy and Janelle shared a glance.

Lucy nodded. Felt as though she had given the

wrong answer. 'And I've been doing some casual work for a small graphic design company.'

This answer seemed to satisfy Janelle.

Lucy wanted them to like her; she wanted to fit in. She looked over Janelle's desk for something to spark a further topic of conversation. There was a poster for a music festival. A column of photos of Janelle with gorgeous, smiling party people. Nothing there Lucy could relate to.

'How long have you worked here?' she asked.

They told her they'd both been at Oracle for a few years each and then the conversation died out. No doubt they both thought *they* should be working on the OZ campaign. And Lucy agreed. They had more right to, since they'd been here longer. And what did Lucy know about doing a major pitch like this?

She had a degree, but little practical experience. Instead of working, designing and learning on the job, she'd been changing nappies, washing clothes and cooking endless batches of spaghetti Bolognese.

People—rude people—sometimes asked if she regretted having Lachie. Of course, in a rare quiet moment she sometimes wondered what her life would have been like if she hadn't had a baby at seventeen, but she could never regret Lachie. He was her world.

Lachie wasn't a mistake, but he was her responsibility. Getting pregnant at seventeen wasn't usually part of anyone's perfect life plan, but Lucy had made that bed, laid in it with her ex, Alex, and now lived with the consequences.

She could never regret Lachie. But that didn't mean she didn't have other regrets. Wishing she'd finished high school *first*. Wishing things had worked out with Alex. Wishing her life hadn't been just that much harder than everyone else's.

Wishing that she'd had a carefree time at university. Been able to go out, party, meet boys…

Oracle was such a modern agency, with a young, carefree workforce. No doubt they all socialised together, went for after-work drinks, talked about dating, holidays they'd been on or were planning and all the things you undoubtedly did if you were young and unburdened by commitment.

She wanted to pretend that she was unencumbered, even for a few hours a day. And she was going to give herself permission not to feel guilty about it. Lachie had been her number one priority for five years. Now she was working and Lachie was at school…maybe…just maybe she could pretend for a while?

Besides, if Marcus knew she was a single mother, would he have given her a chance to work on the OZ Airways pitch? *This is going to consume you… For the next six weeks you'll live and breathe OZ Airways.* If he knew she had other commitments? That, as dedicated as she was, the job could never be her number one priority? Would he have given her this opportunity if he'd have known?

Maybe. Maybe not. Either way, she wasn't prepared to risk it.

Lucy had brought a sandwich from home and ate it at her desk while she found her way around the Oracle IT system. Then she googled 'OZ Airways', 'Travel' and 'Tourism' to get her head into the right space. At three o'clock, they met in Marcus's office. It was no less intimidating than the boardroom, and somehow worse, as it was more intimate, surrounded by Marcus's things. She noticed more now than she had during that first, disorienting interview.

There was a painting that looked like a Bret Whitley. No doubt an original. Framed photographs, all arranged beautifully. Many of them of Marcus surrounded by other people. At a quick scan, he seemed to be standing with Oracle employees. Possibly at awards nights. Parties. Celebrations. There was a print from the wildly successful cereal campaign he'd designed a few years ago. She'd studied that campaign as part of a unit on advertising. Marcus had no less than four large monitors on his two desks, but still carried a state-of-the-art tablet with him wherever he went.

Floor-to-ceiling bookshelves were lined with books of varying sizes, shapes and colours. In addition to the books, on his shelves were a few small sculptures that looked expensive. Some smaller framed photographs were also on the shelves. From a distance they looked like family portraits. Old. But she was too far away to study them closely. And there was a Northern Suburbs cap. That was her team too. She wished she didn't know that Marcus also supported them. In fact, she didn't want to know more about Marcus and his personal life than she absolutely needed to.

'As I said earlier, I don't believe in defined roles. Obviously you and Daphne are designers.' He smiled at Lucy. 'Liam's the market researcher, but we all think, and we all have ideas.' Marcus swivelled his whole body towards Lucy and focused on her. She felt warm. On alert. It wasn't unpleasant—far from it. It was just unfortunate that two other people were looking on as the heat rose up inside her and every muscle in her body waited for what Marcus was going to do or say next.

'I don't have time for egos. If it's the best idea it doesn't matter if it comes from the copywriter or the office manager. We all have our strengths and will be responsible for certain parts of the project, but we'll only win the campaign if we adopt the best ideas.'

Lucy nodded. It made perfect sense to her. Besides, she hadn't had an ego in five years. You didn't put yourself first when a tiny human depended on you for everything.

Marcus continued. 'OZ Airways isn't just an airline—it partners with accommodation providers, tour operators and restaurants so it can position itself as a one-stop travel shop. We aren't just thinking about plane travel, but all aspects of travel from your front door and back again.'

Liam did a brief presentation on the tourism market, trends, and spending habits the types of travellers who used OZ Airways. How those things had changed over the past few years.

Then they spent the next two hours tossing around ideas, the campaigns that had worked in the past and why. The ones that hadn't. She was enjoying herself immensely. Marcus was right: there was no room for egos. After a particularly lively discussion about Paul Hogan's strengths and weaknesses, Lucy looked down at her watch in horror. It had just gone five.

'I'm very sorry, Marcus, but I have to leave. I have an…um appointment.'

He looked at her but didn't say anything. She glanced at the others. Everyone held the same blank expression, their mouths just slightly ajar.

'Is there something I need to do before I go?'

'For tomorrow, I want a draft design or marketing concept, from each of you, not just Lucy. As homework.'

Homework. Right. There was no escaping it even now she'd graduated.

A design concept.

'You'll have it by morning. I'm so sorry,' she muttered as she left the room, not daring to look at their faces. Let alone listen to what they might be saying about her as she closed the door behind herself.

It was mortifying, but the only other choice was equally as mortifying: if she didn't leave the office by five o'clock sharp, she'd be late to collect Lachie from after-school care. The fine for being late would eat into the money she'd make today, and if you were late too often to collect your child, they would cancel the booking and she'd have no one to look after Lachie each afternoon.

Irresponsible teenage mother...

Luckily the trains were running on time and she was heading over the Harbour Bridge and to Lachie by quarter past five.

A whole design concept? By the morning? Was he kidding?

Lucy took out her notebook and started sketching. It wouldn't be her best work, but she could work properly later. Lucy's parents both still worked. Her mother was a pharmacist and her father an accountant. Either of her parents could collect Lachie in an emergency, but Lucy hated to ask them. And if she was already having emergencies on her first day of work, where would it end? No, Lachie was her responsibility. She had relied on them too much already.

She reached Lachie's school just before five thirty. He looked up from the puzzle he was doing with one of the educators at after-school care and beamed when he saw her. Her heart leapt as he jumped up and ran to her, throwing his arms around her. He smelt of school, but still Lachie. She pressed his soft, warm cheek against hers and held him. One day, probably not too far the future, he'd be too embarrassed to hug his mother when she collected him. But for now he needed her hugs every bit as much as she needed his, and all the worries and stress from the day melted away. When Lachie was in her arms, everything was okay.

They took the short bus ride to her parents' house while Lachie told her about his day, how he had won the game of build-up tips at lunchtime and how the class had got some chicken eggs and they were now waiting for them to hatch. Her heart melted when he asked her how her day had gone.

Her mum and dad arrived home not long after Lucy and Lachie.

She cooked dinner for everyone, pasta carbonara with a salad for the adults and carrot and cucumber sticks for Lachie. Lucy listened again as Lachie told his grandparents about the chicken eggs. After dinner, she got Lachie ready for bed and read to him. It was after eight by the time she switched on her laptop and started to properly put together some designs. They weren't well researched, just ideas, and she hoped that would be enough. When the clock ticked over to the next day she finally hit Send.

CHAPTER TWO

'I THOUGHT SHE was an interesting choice,' Daphne murmured. Just loudly enough for only Marcus to hear.

Marcus shook his head. 'She's very talented.'

'I'm sure she is.' Daphne's tone was playful, and she was one of his longest standing and most loyal employees. She wouldn't hesitate to tell him when she thought one of ideas was stupid. Or unworkable. Or a very bad idea.

And she was gently calling him out now.

He'd wanted Lucy before he met her. But not in the way Daphne was implying; he wanted her as part of his *team*. He'd seen some stuff her old firm had put out. It was clever. Witty. Gorgeous.

He'd been keeping an eye on her firm's director and had contemplated making a takeover offer at some stage, but then he'd advertised the junior designer position and Lucy's CV had happened across his desk. Some examples of her work were listed and he'd known she was the designer he wanted.

For the *job*.

She had presented well at interview. Which wasn't a surprise. The fact that she was gorgeous was obvious, but at that moment he'd been focused on convincing her to move across to Oracle. Her work was beautiful, clever, cheeky and with a maturity that belied her age.

Playful, not cynical like your typical twenty-something. In person she was professional. Serious even.

The only thing he could figure out about Lucy Spencer was that she was *not* typical.

The other thing he now saw without any doubt or distraction was that Lucy Spencer was undeniably, unmistakably beautiful. He'd noticed her looks right away—he wasn't blind—but he'd pushed it aside as an irrelevancy. Of course he had. He was a professional and he hired the best person for the job. Just like he wouldn't consider a candidate's age, gender, appearance, race, disabilities or any other matter that was wholly irrelevant to someone's ability to do the job. And the fact was that Lucy had the smoothest skin he'd seen in as long as he could remember. And that her light brown eyes were almost unnaturally round. And if he happened to let himself linger too long on them he might find himself losing track of the conversation he was meant to be participating in. Or even his own name.

The woman he had interviewed two weeks earlier had been gorgeous, for sure, but she'd also been slightly shy and standoffish. It was part of his job to understand human behaviour, so he watched people carefully. Of course he'd noticed her straight, light brown hair, cut into a simple style, sitting just on her shoulders. She was petite and unadorned. He'd liked her instantly and if his pulse had risen, well, that was just because he was glad to be hiring a designer he'd admired from afar.

At this morning's meeting, his heart rate had also increased when she'd walked into the meeting and smiled at him. But he put that down to the fact that he believed he had just added another talented member to his high-performing team. Nothing more or less.

And the fact that his blood started to pump a little harder each time he looked at her? Irrelevant. He'd never put his libido above his job.

Never.

And he wasn't about to now. Not when he was preparing for the biggest pitch of his career.

Today had gone well; he was confident he had assembled the best team for the OZ Airways work. Lucy belonged on the team—even if Daphne had shot him a few warning looks during the meeting to question his motivation in putting a newbie on a team as important as this one. He had wondered for the briefest of moments if Daphne was right. Was he distracted somehow by Lucy? Was she too inexperienced to be part of this sort of campaign?

If you never gave junior staff big opportunities, how would they ever learn?

Besides, she might be new, but she was also the

one with the most to prove. She had to establish herself; she would be hungrier. She would work harder.

'You won't find a harder worker,' Lucy's last boss had told Marcus over the phone.

Which made what had just happened so puzzling.

As Lucy stood, walked out of his office and closed the door behind herself without a backward glance, he wondered if Daphne was right. Had he been noticing the way her lips were perfectly symmetrical and missed something more important? She had walked out of a meeting with barely any explanation. An appointment. She'd said she had an appointment. After five? On her first day at work. Who did that?

'Did she mention this to you?' he asked Daphne.

Daphne pushed her lips and shook her head.

Right.

Marcus was certainly annoyed, but there was something about Lucy's spunk, her bravado, that had him shaking his head in wonder. She was a junior designer, straight out of university on her first day and she'd left a meeting with the CEO to walk out the door at five o'clock sharp? She was either really brave or really stupid. And he thought he already knew enough about Lucy Spencer to know that she wasn't the latter.

His legs twitched and he struggled to stay seated through the remainder of the meeting.

Once Daphne and Liam left, he stood and paced the full length of his office. He looked out the floor-to-ceiling windows, down to the rooftops below. Not for the first time he thought that the plain grey roofs of the shorter office buildings were a wasted advertising space. Sure, they were hardly a billboard on the M5, but if you were entrepreneurial enough...daring enough.

It was definitely daring. Walking out of a meeting with your boss on your first day in a job because you had 'an appointment'. Who left work at 5:00 p.m. anyway? He was sure some people did, but no one at his firm. He never had. Why would you? The traffic was the absolute worst at that time. His limbs felt strange. Buzzing with energy. Like he'd had too much caffeine, but he'd only had his usual two shots that morning. Yet he felt as though he'd just chugged an entire can of energy drink.

Maybe she had a date?

Though his mind should not be going there. It was positively neanderthal. Not to mention unprofessional.

There were many other reasons why she might be leaving at five.

Doctor's appointment? Dentist? Her teeth were beautiful, straight, and white...and no. Wouldn't you rearrange a dental appointment if you were starting a new job?

He had to focus. He moved to his standing desk

and started playing with ideas, looked over Liam's figures and finally, somewhere around seven, got into the flow of work. He ordered dinner from his usual place and had almost forgotten about Lucy and her 'appointment' when he left the office around nine. He took the short walk home to his apartment, a penthouse, overlooking the bay in Woolloomooloo. It was in a small, exclusive building, once a shipping warehouse, now top-end apartments. He had a berth for a yacht if he'd wanted one. His mother had laughed when she'd first seen it. 'It's beautiful, but it's the sort of apartment for someone who is actually going to spend some time there enjoying the view. Maybe I could move in and you could move back to the North Shore?'

His mother was joking—the townhouse he'd bought her was gorgeous and her view of the harbour no less impressive than his. But her point about not ever being in the apartment to enjoy the view was a valid one.

Never mind, the view from his office was equally inspiring and he wasn't yet at a point in his career where he could afford to sit back, feet up, sipping cocktails and looking at any view. He certainly wasn't at the point in his career where he would contemplate sharing his life with someone. He had nothing of himself left over to give to a woman. A partner was not part of Marcus Hawke's plan. He had flings—he wasn't celibate—but he was careful to be clear about the boundaries he had in place around those flings: no falling in love. He couldn't promise a future.

Marcus slept badly, returning to consciousness every hour or so. The pressure of the OZ Airways pitch was going to get to him at some stage; he just hadn't expected it to happen so soon. His alarm went off at six as usual and, as always, the first thing he did was pick up his phone and check his messages.

At two past midnight this morning Lucy Spencer had sent him an email. Her draft design concepts.

His fingers felt strange as he opened the attachments. Shaky somehow. Low blood sugar levels probably.

Even on the small screen he could see the designs were amazing. Rough, to be sure, but inspired. Three completely different approaches.

He sighed loudly and fell back against his pillows. What was her story?

After his usual workout on the rowing machine and treadmill, he showered and dressed. All the time trying to figure out why on earth Lucy would have left the office so suddenly and then gone home to work until midnight.

You don't need to know her life story; you just need to win the OZ account.

It was perfectly possible to do that without

knowing what made Lucy Spencer tick. Or what she did outside work.

A life outside work? Did people have those anymore? Not Marcus and not most of his staff.

His work was his life—and his life was his work. You didn't become the most influential changer of hearts, minds and behaviours by having hobbies. You didn't win the most important advertising campaigns by sailing your yacht. You didn't change harmful habits and behaviours by sitting back and enjoying the view.

Marcus arrived at the office just before eight and Tara was waiting with his coffee and breakfast: egg-and-bacon roll and a large cappuccino. See, that was the sort of dedication he received from his staff. He ate his breakfast, drank his coffee and focused on his work until, just before nine, a movement down the corridor made him look up from his screen.

His chest rose, then ashamed of his reaction, instantly dropped. He had proofs to focus on, not the gorgeous brunette who was currently walking up the corridor to her cubicle, greeting her colleagues with a warm smile. She was wearing low heels and a light blue dress that flicked ever so slightly behind her as she turned to sit at her desk.

Awkward.

Where had she gone last night? Yoga? Her posture was good enough. A beauty appointment? No. Somehow he sensed Lucy's beauty was natural.

Then what?

It didn't matter, that was *what*. Lucy Spencer was not part of his current plan.

In the ten years he'd been working in advertising, he had never dated a colleague. Never gone there. Oracle Creative didn't have a strict no-fraternising-with-colleagues policy; that would be unfair to his staff. They worked long hours, devoted most of their waking hours to the job. It would be unworkable—not to mention cruel—to prohibit personal relationships between his employees. But he had some rules. Rules to make sure relationships were absolutely consensual. Rules to make sure everyone was safe and happy.

Those were the rules that applied to his staff.

The rule he applied to himself was even stricter.

He turned back to the proofs.

Midmorning, Marcus heard the commotion but ignored it and continued writing the email he was working on. A few people left their desks to investigate but the noise became louder. He was considering closing his office door to block out the noise when a shriek cut through above the other noise and he jumped to his feet. He followed the others, heading towards the office kitchen. Marcus overtook them all and saw the source of the shrieking was Amy. The cause of her shrieks was an unconscious Janelle, sprawled out on the kitchen floor. Blood was splattered over her chest and Lucy was standing over her.

His throat closed over and a cool sweat erupted over his body. 'What's going on?' he managed to whisper.

'Everyone back,' Lucy said, calmly, yet with volume and authority. Marcus stood where he was. Frozen.

'You too, Marcus. Make sure Amy's okay, but please don't let her back in here. Tell her Janelle will be fine.'

When he didn't move, Lucy touched his shoulder and pushed him gently back. Her warm touch jolted him out of his inertia. He coughed to clear his throat.

'Would someone tell me what on earth is going on?' he said, sounding a bit too much like he was panicking for his liking.

'Janelle was cutting an apple and sliced her hand. Badly. Then Amy screamed and now Janelle has fainted. Does anyone know if Janelle has any underlying health conditions?'

He still couldn't move. There was a lot of blood. So much blood. It couldn't just have come from her hand. Lucy crouched down with a towel and wrapped it around Janelle's hand. She tried to rouse Janelle by gently stroking her head.

'Marcus, does she have any underlying medical issues?' Lucy prompted again.

He shook his head. He had no idea. 'Could

someone please find a cushion or something?'
Lucy asked.

His limbs were weak. Shaky. *Pull yourself together, man.*

Daphne turned and left—to fulfil Lucy's orders, he hoped. Just then, Janelle started to slowly regain consciousness. Lucy spoke softly. 'Welcome back, how are you feeling?'

Janelle murmured and tried to sit.

'Relax. You've just fainted. And you cut your hand, but you're going to be fine. You're probably going to need some stitches. Would you like me to take you to the hospital?'

'Ambulance!' Marcus said.

Janelle moaned. Daphne came back with a cushion from the couch. Lucy slid it under Janelle's legs.

'Shouldn't you put that under her head?' he asked.

Lucy shot him a look that he would have described as exasperated. No one, except his mother, had looked at him like that for years. She didn't even respond but turned back to Janelle.

'It's up to you. If you relax and can stand we can probably just get a cab. You've just had a fright.'

'Has someone called an ambulance?' Marcus asked again.

'I have,' said Daphne, appearing again behind him.

He noticed a wry grin on Lucy's face and he knew that she believed an ambulance was overkill.

'I'm her employer, I have duties to her and I say we call an ambulance.'

Lucy shrugged and turned back to her patient. 'I'm thirsty,' Janelle said.

'Okay, but just a little. In case they want to take you into surgery. Hopefully it will just need stitches, but if they have to operate you'll get in quicker if you haven't eaten or drunk anything. You did quite a good job of it.' Lucy looked down at Janelle and smiled.

Janelle nodded. Almost smiled back.

'Are you sure it's just her hand? There's so much...blood.' Marcus hated the way he couldn't properly enunciate the last word.

'It's just her hand, and as long as we keep the pressure on, it'll be fine. How's Amy?'

'She's calmed down. She's just had a fright too.'

When the paramedics arrived about ten minutes later, Janelle was sitting and Lucy handed her care over. She joined him at the kitchen door. Oblivious to the blood that was on her own dress.

So. Much. Blood.

'I'm sorry about your dress. We'll pay for it to get dry cleaned.'

Lucy laughed. 'It's fine. It'll wash out. I don't own anything that needs dry-cleaning.'

Marcus didn't do blood. He didn't know if that had happened since he was fourteen or whether it had been before that. If he'd been the first in the kitchen he might have screamed just like Amy.

'Are you okay?' she asked.

'Fine,' he snapped and his body flushed with shame.

'You just look pale, that's all. When did you eat last?'

'I'm fine, really,' he replied. This time more softly.

Lucy scrunched up her face and appeared hurt. It was unkind of him to snap, especially when Lucy had been the only one in the office to have her wits about her.

She turned to leave and he fought the desire to pull her back.

'Will you go with her? To the hospital?'

She turned and smiled. Another kind of sensation flooded his veins.

'If she wants me to, of course,' she said.

'I think you're the only one who's calm enough.'

Lucy frowned and when she did a little crease appeared between her eyes. The only crease on an otherwise blemish-free face.

'Were you a nurse in a past life?' he asked.

She laughed and shook her head. 'No.' She reached out and placed her palm gently on his arm and he felt the last drops of blood leave his head. 'You should have something to drink. A juice or something—you really do look pale.'

He wasn't all right, but couldn't tell Lucy that.

Janelle's blood in the kitchen was one thing. But Lucy's warm hand on his arm was what was unsettling him most. One small gentle touch was ricocheting through him like lightning. Simultaneously he wanted to brush her away and pull her closer. In the end, she made the decision for him, lifting her hand and crouching back down to Janelle.

Once the paramedics had assured him that Janelle would be fine and had kindly lied and told everyone that they hadn't overreacted by calling an ambulance, he went back to his office and the email he'd been drafting.

Lucy had been calm. Authoritative, even though she was the newest team member and possibly the youngest.

He closed his eyes and placed his hand over them, but Lucy's image still hung before his eyelids. Holding Janelle's hand tightly with one hand, her hand on Janelle's shoulder with the other.

It was ridiculous. He was just stressed. And was it any wonder?

The OZ account would be the biggest his agency had ever had. If they won it—and it was a success—it would cement his firm as one of Australia's best. He already had a reputation as 'innovative' and 'cutting edge'. Unfortunately, the critics also used terms like 'maverick' and 'risk taker', which would've made him laugh if it wasn't so important to be taken seriously. Marcus was actually one of the most risk-averse people he knew. 'Fresh', 'new kid on the block'—he could live with those descriptions, except what he wanted was adjectives like 'respected' and 'trusted'. Because if you were going to change the way people behaved, they had to trust you.

OZ Airways was one of the highest profile advertisers in the country. Some of their previous campaigns had been truly iconic and lingered in the national psyche. But most importantly, a campaign like this would let him lead the others. The serious ones.

Health.

Smoking.

Drinking.

Driving.

That was his plan and the plan was right on track.

And Lucy Spencer was not going to lead him off it.

CHAPTER THREE

SHE HOPED IT would get easier over time. By Friday morning of her first week Lucy was a wreck of nervous energy. Learning a new job was exhausting, and working into the night on Monday and then again Wednesday had been shattering. Then there were the usual things: getting Lachie ready for school, cooking, washing, getting Lachie to bed. But she was determined to do this.

It may have all been manageable, were it not for the additional pressure of pretending that she fitted in to Oracle Creative. The other employees were mostly young, just like her. *Unlike* her, they were mostly unattached. They were interesting, sharp dressers. With hair coloured in untraditional shades. She was learning to guess which department someone worked in by the way they were dressed: the creatives, the designers and the copywriters wore edgy, trendy outfits, had groomed eyebrows and statement earrings. The brand strategists preferred jeans and T-shirts emblazoned with pithy or ironic quotes.

The media buyers were the only cohort who wore suits, and even then, not on Fridays, as she noticed today.

When Lucy had got the call to let her know she had the job, she'd treated herself to a shopping spree, but the clothes she'd bought favoured functionality over flair. Some well-cut black and blue pants, a few patterned blouses and cotton shirts. Before she had Lachie, she had the time and energy to put interesting outfits together; she had even sewn occasionally. Now all her creative energy went into her work.

And the lies she was having to tell on a daily basis.

Lying was *exhausting*.

She had lots of appointments. Every night it seemed. Her colleagues were probably beginning to think she had a serious medical condition.

She toyed with the idea of coming clean with Marcus. Surely her position was safe; she was on the special team he'd put together for the OZ pitch. The few comments he'd made to her indicated he was happy with the work she'd done so far. As well as her commitment.

Midmorning, she noticed Marcus was in his office. His door was wide open and she could see him at his computer, his blue eyes focused on the screen, his posture alert but relaxed. There didn't seem to be any meetings or frantic deadlines looming and she'd taken a sip of water and a deep breath. As she stood she caught a glimpse of a new photo on Amy's partition. In it, Amy was holding a chubby-cheeked baby, about six months old or so, Lucy guessed. The sight of a gorgeous chubby baby always made Lucy's heart swell, reminding her of her own soft-cheeked cherub.

'Gorgeous baby,' Lucy said. 'Is she yours?'

Amy snorted. 'Oh, no way. That's my niece. My sister's *a lot* older than me.'

Lucy froze. 'Oh, okay. Sure. Um, does anyone here have kids?'

Amy shook her head. 'Nope. Actually, you know Genevieve did, but she left. Advertising is a young person's game, isn't it? Work hard, party harder.'

Lucy nodded, unable to reply further. She walked away, but to the bathrooms, not Marcus's office as she'd originally planned.

In the bathroom, she went into an empty cubicle, lowered the seat and sat while she breathed deeply and let her heart rate return to normal levels. So what if no one else had kids? She would be the first. She *was* the first, whether they knew about Lachie or not. She'd always been the first. The first—and only—girl at her selective school to have a baby. Probably still the only one. Her classmates had all gone straight onto university, just like Alex. And just like Alex, they had barely looked back.

Lucy went back to her desk without another word.

While she believed that outwardly, at least, Marcus would be understanding if he knew about Lachie, she also knew that something would change. That the air between them wouldn't be as charged. That he wouldn't look at her the way he had been looking at her all week, with curiosity and a dash of desire.

No one had looked at her like that. Not for years.

Not that anything could ever happen between her and Marcus—that was so far out of the realm of any possibility, it was laughable. There was more chance that one of the Hemsworth brothers would appear and ask her out. Marcus was her boss and she wasn't about to do anything to jeopardise her and Lachie's future. But that didn't mean she couldn't enjoy the way he noticed her. It didn't mean she also couldn't enjoy the view up the long corridor to his office, of Marcus, his dark head concentrating over one of his screens or running his hands through his thick dark hair as he spoke to someone on the phone.

They could look, but not touch. There was no harm in a bit of admiration.

By her third week at Oracle, Lucy had pushed the decision to tell Marcus about Lachie to one side. They were busy with the pitch and she didn't want to distract from that. She was at her desk, working on some designs, trying different colour combinations and layouts.

'Lucy?'

She turned, startled. She had to learn not to

react like that whenever Marcus spoke to her. But something about the way his deep voice vibrated in her chest, at just the right frequency, made the muscles deep in her chest quiver.

'Am I that frightening?'

You've no idea...

'Just in my own world, that's all.'

'Can you pop into my office for a moment? I want to go over the presentation with you all and iron out some bugs.'

Lucy, Liam and Daphne sat with Marcus in his office and refined and finessed the speech he would give. She loved the way he collaborated with his team and the way he considered every idea carefully. Lucy was becoming more and more confident to speak up with her thoughts, knowing she wouldn't be shouted down, even if her idea was silly. Marcus didn't judge anyone on the basis of one bad idea, but encouraged his team to look at something from a different angle.

In so many respects he seemed like an island. He lived alone—staff gossip had confirmed that Marcus was single. She didn't get the impression he had much of an existence beyond his work. He was one of the first to arrive each morning and the last to leave. The team at Oracle seemed to be his best friends. Maybe even his family as well. Lucy was in awe of his ambition, but yet...

'The presentation is at nine, so I think we should all be in by eight at the latest.'

He looked around the room but his eyes stopped on Lucy. Why was he looking at her in particular?

'Do you want me to come?' she asked.

'Of course.'

'Oh.'

'I'll do the bulk of the talking, but they want to meet the team. And besides, you've been an important part of this project. You deserve to be there. Plus, it'll be a great experience.'

Their gazes locked. His expression fell from eagerness to concern. She realised how a koala must feel in the middle of the road in the path of an oncoming car.

'Is there a problem?' he asked.

'No, not at all. I just didn't realise.' Her mind was spinning with the logistics required in getting to the office by eight and getting Lachie to school just before nine.

'Good. It will be fun.'

Daphne and Liam laughed. At this moment, presenting to the OZ Airways advertising department didn't feel exactly like 'fun'. It felt like her insides were being tossed in a whirlpool.

Lucy's father was happy to drop Lachie at school, but Lucy still felt guilty as she got on the train at seven fifteen. She was even in before either Daphne or Liam. After placing her bag on her desk, she walked slowly up to Marcus's room and poked her head around the door. He was standing at the window, with his back to her, looking over the city. His arms were at his sides, and by the way his shoulders rose and fell gently she guessed he was taking deep breaths. For a few quiet moments she just enjoyed the pleasure of watching him, tall, broad, silhouetted by the rising sun streaming through the floor-to-ceiling windows.

The skin on the back of his neck alone was worthy of several minutes of careful study: smooth and lightly tanned. She bet it tasted delicious. She batted that thought away as quickly as it came. His long neck met his short, light brown hair. It was cut well, into a style that allowed it to look good, even without combing...

Suddenly, he turned. Damn. Caught.

But he smiled broadly. 'Lucy, Lucy, come in.'

'Please tell me you went home and haven't been here all night,' she teased.

'Why, do I look crumpled?'

'No! Not at all, you look wonderful.' *Damn*... 'I just meant you were here late, you're here early and...'

He grinned, a gorgeous, knowing grin that didn't stop the redness growing across her cheeks, only exacerbated it.

'Sit down, have some coffee.' He pointed to a pot on his desk.

The smell hit her nostrils and she gratefully

accepted. He sat across from her and poured her a cup.

'It's going to be great. You're so well prepared.'

'Thank you, Lucy. I'll feel fine once I get going, but the few moments beforehand can be nerve-racking. It's too late to change much, but you keep wondering if you should.'

'I understand completely. Do you want to go over it again or have you been doing that all night?'

He laughed. 'The latter. Just do me a favour.'

'Anything.'

'Just talk to me. Distract me. How are you finding things at Oracle?'

'Great, just great.'

'Fitting in okay?'

What was he suggesting? That he knew she was a square peg in a round hole?

'Just fine. Everyone's been great.'

'Janelle was very grateful for your help the other week.'

'It was nothing.'

'No, it was something. And I was very grateful too. You kept calm while the rest of us over-reacted. It was very mature of you.'

Her chest warmed. But that was probably just the coffee she was sipping.

'I've done a first aid course, that's all.' She couldn't believe she was the only one in the office who had, but if she hadn't had Lachie, she may not have spent a Saturday at the St John's Ambulance offices learning about heart attacks and snake bites either.

'More of us should do one,' he conceded. 'Maybe as an office team building exercise.'

She nodded. 'That's a good idea.'

Marcus sipped his coffee, then placed it down carefully. 'Are you sure you're finding everything okay?'

What did he know? She should just come clean. This was the perfect opportunity. But she nodded. She could hardly tell him about Lachie an hour before the pitch. 'Everything's fine.'

'There's nothing else we can do for you, to make anything easier?'

Oh, God, he *knew*.

'I'm good.' She could just tell him. If there was a moment, it was now or never.

She looked him straight in the eyes.

Big mistake.

He looked straight at her, and the rest of the world dropped away.

'Do you have a long commute, or do you live nearby?' he asked.

No, he didn't know, but he was fishing. He was trying to figure out why she was leaving on the dot of five most days.

'North. Um, Artarmon.' It was a twenty-minute train ride from the city. Thirty from the office to the school. She'd practiced it before she even got the job.

'Convenient,' he replied, and she couldn't help but laugh. It wasn't a long commute. She was lucky; many people had much further to travel. But she'd bet he had far less.

'And where do you live?'

The corners of his pink lips tugged upward.

He nodded to the east, in the direction of the eastern suburbs. 'Potts Point? Elizabeth Bay?' she guessed.

'Woolloomooloo,' he answered. It was even closer. You could probably see his place from where they stood.

'Convenient,' she said, and he laughed.

'So what do you do in your spare time?' Marcus asked.

Lucy wrinkled her nose and gave a wry chuckle. She couldn't remember the last time she had time for herself.

'What's so funny?'

'Nothing, sorry. It's just… I've been focused on studying, you know. But I read, listen to music when I can. What do you like to do in your spare time?'

'I suppose I don't get much spare time either,' Marcus smiled. 'But I'm a reader too.'

They realised they had similar taste in music and that he had read the book she was currently reading last month. They also followed the same podcasts. *It's bad enough he's so handsome, why does he have to be nice as well?* They were talking about the latest episode when Daphne knocked on the door.

'Good morning, team. Ready to pitch?'

Liam joined them shortly afterwards and they all went over the presentation together one more time. At eight thirty, Marcus declared, 'Let's go team,' and headed to the elevator. Lucy quickly grabbed her bag and laptop from her desk. She had to take extra quick steps to catch up with Marcus's long strides.

On the street, Marcus hailed a cab. His long arm authoritatively made a car cross over two lanes of traffic to collect them. Tall, lean and confident. The world seemed to do whatever Marcus Hawke wanted.

Lucy had never been present at a provisional pitch before, so had nothing to compare it to, but judging by the way they were taking notes and the smiles on their faces, Lucy felt they were impressed. She didn't know if that meant they were successful, but she did know they had done a great job. By the time they were shown out, Lucy was exhausted and she'd only watched and made polite small talk with the OZ advertising team.

Daphne and Liam caught the first elevator, but as it was already quite full, Marcus and Lucy waited for the next. Once they were inside and alone, they both exhaled loudly. Noticing their tandem sighs, they looked at each other and laughed.

'Are you glad it's over?' she asked.

'Oh, yes. What did you think?' Marcus asked.

'I think they liked it.'

'Why do you say that?' He was asking for details, not challenging her.

'You were talking and concentrating on the director, but I was looking around the room. They were taking notes, sharing quick looks. They were trying not to give anything away. If they hated it, they wouldn't risk looking at one another. They were nice people and that would be rude. So, they liked it.' As soon as she finished speaking she felt foolish. Would Marcus understand her reasoning or was she totally off base?

Marcus cocked his head to one side and studied her. As the elevator plunged down to street level, so did her stomach. 'You're right. Great observation. How did you get to be so good at judging human behaviour?'

She didn't know what to say at that point. Her mouth was dry and she probably couldn't have got any words out even if her brain could choose some.

Luckily the doors spread open before she had to.

Every Friday night the entire office went for after-work drinks at a nearby bar. Lachie was due to spend this weekend with his father. For once

Lucy could be the one to go out on the town, socialise with her colleagues and not worry about what time she got home.

For once, she could be Lucy Spencer, graphic designer. Not Loser Lucy, teenage mother. Not Lachie's Mum.

The rest of the day passed quickly. Ironically enough, the day she didn't have to rush off was the day everyone else was ready to leave the office before five.

'No appointment today?' Daphne smirked.

'Nope.' Lucy smiled as best she could and shook her head.

She felt light as she grabbed her things and shut her computer down. Alex should be picking Lachie up shortly and she had the evening free. For a few hours, at least, she could be just like Amy and Janelle and everyone else in the office and just relax into the feeling of having no commitments whatsoever.

Lucy followed Amy and Marcus to a bar just around the corner which was already heaving with office workers. The walls were lined with mirrors, and the bar several people deep. 'I'll get the drinks,' Marcus said to Amy. 'See if you can find us a table?'

Lucy squeezed past men in suits and women in sleek dresses and high heels and followed Amy to the back of the bar, where Daphne and Liam had found a booth. A bottle of champagne and

an ice bucket and glasses sat on the table in front
of them. Lucy slid into the booth next to Daphne.
It was hard to hear the conversation over fifty
other conversations and loud music. But Lucy
didn't care.

Moments later Marcus appeared with another
bottle of champagne and three more glasses. He
slid into the booth next to Lucy. It wasn't a wide
booth and Lucy was faced with the choice of getting closer to Daphne or enjoying the fact that
Marcus's strong thigh was now pushed resolutely
against her own. They were even more perks to
Friday-night drinks than she had first realised.
Marcus passed her a glass of champagne and their
fingers brushed. She tried to ignore the tingling
sensation that spread through her hand, but she
looked in dismay as her glass shook slightly when
Marcus clinked his glass to hers. 'To a job well
done,' Marcus said and raised his glass to the
table.

'A job well done,' they all echoed. Lucy's chest
warmed and her muscles began to relax. She had
survived her first three weeks and her first presentation to a prospective client and come out the
other end with a glass of champagne in one hand
and her hot boss pressed against her other side.
Not a bad result.

The room was loud, and that wasn't even to
mention the drum beat of her own heart, pound-
ing louder than the music. Rocking, shaking,

destabilising. She looked over and noticed the way the dark fabric of Marcus's trousers strained against the muscles in his thighs. She itched to place her hand on the thigh next to her and see if it was as firm as it appeared. But that would be all types of inappropriate. She tried to concentrate on the conversation, the questions he was asking her.

'Weekend plans?' he asked.

'Nothing,' she said with complete honesty. Before she'd graduated, Lachie's weekends with Alex had been dedicated study time. Now, apart from a couple of loads of washing, she really did have nothing to do. The thought was exciting. Also strange. 'What about you?'

'Work,' he replied. She raised an eyebrow. 'But I'll also see my mother.'

'Did you grow up in Sydney?' she asked, even though Google had already told her the answer.

'Yep.'

'And your father, does he still live here?'

Marcus looked at her briefly but then turned his attention to Amy. Maybe he hadn't heard her.

Or he didn't want to answer.

Lucy felt her phone buzzing in her pocket. The first thing that leapt to mind, as always, was Lachie. 'Alex Rankin' flashed on the screen. *Oh, no.*

She had no way of possibly hearing him in this noise. 'I'm really sorry, Marcus, I need to get this call,' she said and he slid out of the booth. She ignored the way his azure eyes appraised her. Her cheeks burnt as she made her way through the crowded bar and back to the street, where she called Alex back. She knew what he was going to ask before he even said it. It was five minutes to five. She'd make it to after-school care in time, but she shouldn't have to. It was Alex's turn to collect Lachie.

'Client drinks, it's really important. You don't mind if I get him in the morning, do you?'

'I'm at work drinks too, Alex.'

'Yeah, but you've only just started. I've got a lot riding on this.'

So do I.

'It's your weekend with Lachie.' She hated, *hated*, having to convince her son's father to see him. Alex only took Lachie for one weekend a fortnight. It was hardly onerous. Despite saying that he'd spend more time with Lachie once he was older, Alex was still sticking to his fortnightly weekends. And sometimes, like now, he even reneged on those. Her heart cracked each time she had to tell Lachie that he wouldn't be seeing his father. 'Lachie is expecting you. He's looking forward to seeing you.' She resisted the urge to add *God only knows why.*

'He'll understand. Besides, I'll get him in the morning. Lucy, these drinks are with our biggest client. It's not fun—it's work. Look, I'll drop him to school Monday morning. You can have Sunday night to yourself.'

Sunday night, whoopee. What was a Sunday night? It wasn't a Friday.

A few hours later, once Lachie was asleep, Lucy's father handed her a glass of red wine. She thought of the half-drunk glass of champagne she'd left at the bar and the look on Marcus's face as she'd excused herself to leave. His brow lowered, his eyes dark. He wasn't angry; that was the wrong word. But he was definitely suspicious.

Why wouldn't he be? *You've been lying to him for the past three weeks.*

'Your first big presentation. You've earned it,' her father said. They sat together in the living room, the television set to Friday-night crime, with the volume turned low. 'How was it?'

'Exhausting.' After two sips of the wine her limbs were extra heavy. It wouldn't be long before she was in bed as well. Fast asleep.

'You've been working late.'

'I have to.' Lucy tucked her feet under herself and looked at the television.

'Really? He's working you that hard already? You've only just started.'

'Yes, no, not exactly. I feel so bad about leaving at five every day—'

'The time you're meant to finish,' her mother added.

Lucy sighed and turned to face her parents. 'Sure, but no one else does. They're all still there, working until late. I have to prove myself. I have to show them I'm not lazy.'

Her parents exchanged a quick look.

'But your boss, Marcus, he knows you have to pick up Lachie, right?'

Lucy looked at her lap.

'Luce,' her father's voice warned.

'I really, really wanted the job! OC is the best agency in the city and I got an interview! I didn't think it would matter if I didn't tell, but now I'm in too deep.'

'It hasn't been long—you can just tell him. Casually,' her mother suggested.

Marcus had already given her several opportunities to let him know she had a son. How would she just drop something like that into the conversation now? *Here are the new proofs you wanted and by the way I have to go pick up my son.* It had gone on too long for her to just casually drop something like that in.

She shook her head.

'Are you afraid that they might sack you if you tell them about Lachie? Because they can't do that, you know.'

'I know. Technically they can't.'

'They can't. Full stop.'

She drew in a deep breath and let it out in a defeated sigh. 'I want to fit in. I'm not ashamed of Lachie, but…' *For the first time in as long as I can remember I'm not the girl who got knocked up at seventeen. Who flunked out of school.* 'They're all so carefree, they wouldn't understand.'

And it wasn't because of Marcus either. No.

She could never be with someone who was more devoted to his career than he was to her.

Forget Marcus. He will never want to be with you. Especially not once he finds out you were a teenage mother.

CHAPTER FOUR

She had to leave.

An appointment.

On a *Friday* night.

A realisation chilled him and chased away the very last of the warm lust that had settled inside him the moment he had sat next to her in the booth.

She had a boyfriend. *Of course she has a boyfriend—you didn't seriously think someone as lovely as her would be single?*

Disappointment followed by a realisation that hit him like a cold blast.

She had a boyfriend who was telling her to leave. Was the boyfriend controlling her?

Daphne raised her eyebrows as soon as Lucy's back was turned and Marcus was sitting back in the booth, but thankfully she didn't say anything further.

Marcus stayed at the pub for a few more rounds before finding an excuse to leave. It was important to socialise with your staff regularly, but it was also important to know when to leave. He knew his staff respected him, but that didn't mean they didn't need to let off steam and have the occasional rant about work without their boss listening in.

He went home, ordered dinner in, and went to put on some music. As he did, he remembered the conversation he'd had with Lucy the other day. She wasn't a big television watcher; she preferred to listen to music too. Searching through his playlists, he chose one of the artists Lucy had mentioned and felt the tension in his shoulders loosen.

The next morning, after a few hours of work, he got his Tesla out of the garage and went to visit his mother.

Veronica Hawke had been a teacher, but after her eldest son had died she decided to study counselling. She now worked at a community centre with women leaving violent relationships. There was no need for Veronica to work, but working gave her purpose. And kept her mind off other things. Marcus knew exactly how she felt. They had all searched for reasons behind his brother, Joel's, death. And then they had searched for distraction. Marcus's father had never found either. Maybe because the only place he ever looked was the bottom of a whiskey bottle.

As usual, Marcus's mother had laid out a delicious, colourful spread on her balcony. Bright salad and fresh seafood from the fish market. Their Saturday-afternoon ritual, with a glass of crisp wine.

Ever since Lucy had left abruptly last night, the thought that she might be in some sort of abusive relationship had been niggling at him. His mother was the perfect person to ask for advice.

'What should I do if I thought a woman at work was in an abusive relationship?' Apart from finding him and smashing him to a pulp, which Marcus suspected would probably be counter-productive.

'What makes you think she's in an abusive relationship?'

'She keeps leaving early, at a moment's notice. She gets a phone call and is gone. She seems...on edge. I know she's hiding something.'

'Have you met her partner?'

He shook his head. 'No. And...' Technically he didn't even know she was in a relationship.

'Does she live with this person?'

'I don't know.'

His mother gave him a funny look. 'Do you know anything at all about the person she's seeing? Their name?'

Marcus held his hands up in defeat. 'Okay, I'm not even sure she's seeing someone—it's just a hunch. But what else could it be?'

Veronica laughed. 'Is it simply possible she has a life and doesn't want to be beholden to the whole Oracle Creative Cult?'

'What do you mean, Oracle Creative Cult?'

'Work hard, party harder. Marcus, you're a workaholic and you've raised a firm of minions in your shadow. And before you start, I'm not saying there's necessarily anything wrong with that, but did you simply consider the possibility that this woman wants to just get to work, do her job and get home again? Not everyone has to be best friends with everyone they work with. Not everyone wants to work the hours you do.'

He supposed that was possible. But if Lucy was asserting her employment rights, why would she log on each night. Or email him at midnight?

'Other people have lives, hobbies, friends. Family. They go to the gym, meet for drinks or a meal. Normal people leave the office before ten occasionally.'

Marcus didn't like how she stressed 'normal' but he replied, 'I don't believe you,' with a smile so she'd know he was kidding.

'Marcus, darling, you might be joking, but I'm being serious. Yor life lacks balance. I'm not saying you should get married—heavens, you're nowhere near ready for that kind of upheaval—but just...' She smiled and added, 'Have a bit of fun.'

Things must be seriously wrong with his life if his mother was telling him to get laid.

When it came to dating, Marcus had one simple rule: manage expectations. Never let the woman believe that he was after anything more than casual. Never let her believe that casual would change to permanent.

All the studies and statistics showed that in order to excel in your chosen career you had to choose one or two things to do well. No one could be a successful advertiser, a good boss, a good friend, a good son, a good partner and a good father. If you wanted to excel at something, to be the world's best, then you had to sacrifice everything else.

He was a successful advertiser. He managed a good firm. He was good son. That, he figured, was just about enough. For as long as he could remember, that was all he wanted. And he was so close to getting there.

'Why don't you start by asking her if she has a partner?'

'Can I...? I mean, directly? I'm her boss—she might tell me it's none of my business.'

'She might, but I'm sure you can find a way to bring it up carefully. And her response might be illuminating. I'm sure you can think of a way. It's not as though you're the creative mind of the new decade, is it?' She grinned playfully.

He *would* figure out a way to ask, but he wasn't sure he wanted to know.

But by eleven Monday morning, he had lost his nerve. The OZ Airways team were sitting around the table in his office, planning their next steps, in case they were invited to present to the board.

Lucy sat directly opposite him, wearing a pink blouse and smelling like something floral. Something fresh.

He hadn't been this distracted by a woman in

years. And never by a colleague. He had to get a grip on this. He hardly knew her. He was intrigued by her, but that wasn't the same thing as liking her. Or actually knowing her.

You could get to know her.

He had tried that, small talk, gentle questioning. He knew she liked to read crime novels, liked piano music and that she followed the Northern Suburbs like he did, but he didn't know anything about her life. He knew her eyes were a light golden brown and her lips a dusty, distracting pink that probably tasted as delicious as they looked.

But he didn't know if she had a partner. Or whether they were controlling or abusive. His mother's insistence that he was probably overreacting had calmed him. Somewhat. But he couldn't shake the feeling she was keeping something from him.

She certainly had a work ethic; she might leave the office at 5:00 p.m. every day, but he'd never seen her take a lunchbreak. And she always turned her work in on time.

Her work had a rare quality about it: original, sensitive. And wise. If he could get to know her, then maybe he wouldn't find her so fascinating. She'd turn out to be just like every other woman he knew, and he could go back to concentrating on the pitch and the meeting he was meant to be running.

There was a knock at the door and he waved

Tara in. 'I'm sorry to interrupt, but I thought you might want to read the email you've just received from the head of advertising at OZ Airways.' Tara couldn't stop grinning, which reassured him the news was probably good. He opened his emails to find a message inviting his team to formally present to the board in a month and in the meantime to experience OZ Airways for themselves. Enclosed were two business class tickets to Fiji and two to Bali, as well as details of full luxury weekend escapes.

He looked at the team carefully, digesting the message and its consequences.

'There's been a development. OZ has made us a very generous offer.'

'I want to go to Bali!' said Daphne and Liam simultaneously once Marcus had explained.

'Jinx!' they cried.

Marcus looked at Lucy. Did he imagine it or did some of the colour leave her face? Daphne and Liam seemed so intent to take the Bali tickets and they were good friends. He'd need to invent a bloody good reason not to send them to Bali. But could he go to Fiji for a weekend with Lucy? Did he even have a choice?

CHAPTER FIVE

Lucy looked at Marcus standing by the window. It was smattered with raindrops and below him the city was grey and drab.

His eyes held hers. Questioning. She avoided his gaze and answering the question. But focusing on his chest was almost as bad. She tried not to think about how nicely his shoulders filled out the blue business shirt that stretched just right over them. A swimmer's shoulders. Or a rower's. Or just a blessing from the genetic Gods.

He was waiting for her to answer the Fiji question. She didn't need this. Just like she didn't need to know that he smelt like citrus and fresh mint. And man.

'What do you think, Lucy? It's a great opportunity. Do you think you'd be okay to go with me to Fiji?'

Lucy closed her eyes and counted to three because surely when she opened them she'd find herself at home in bed waking up from a very strange dream. She took a deep breath, exhaled, then opened her eyes, but Marcus, his spectacular office and his well-fitting shirt were still all in front of her.

'When?' she asked.

'The email said this weekend,' Daphne interrupted. 'You'd fly to Nadi Friday morning. Stay around there for a night and go out to one of the islands for the next night.'

Marcus's lips tilted in an awkward, and she thought perhaps slightly shy, smile.

How was she going to get out of this? She didn't want to be rude or insubordinate, but there was no way she could just drop everything and go away for a weekend.

'And we'll get the red-eye to Bali Thursday night. What do you say, Liam? The beach or the mountains? Seminyak or Ubud?'

'Oh, beach, definitely the beach.'

'But I hear Ubud is wonderful. Or Munduk,' Daphne said.

'Why me? Why take me?' Lucy said softly.

'Why not you?' Daphne turned to her.

Oh, dear, there were so many reasons why not her, none of which she wanted to explain. Unless she absolutely had to.

'I guess I'm worried the others will be upset. I've only been here a few weeks.'

'That's true,' Marcus said. 'It's admirable you're worried about staff morale and perceptions. But the others have all enjoyed perks at some point or another. Besides, leave them to me—I can smooth things over.'

Lucy was too stunned at Marcus's generosity as boss to come back with a persuasive reply. 'But for the weekend, is it worth it, going all that way?'

'I know it's only two nights, but it's a great opportunity to truly get our heads around the client's business.'

Only two nights?

It would be two nights away from Lachie, three full days given that she probably wouldn't see him again until the Monday morning. Three days she had to count on her parents to look after her son. She had promised herself all those years ago that Lachie was her responsibility she wasn't going to take advantage of the parents any more than she absolutely had to.

Unfortunately, it wasn't Alex's weekend to take Lachie. If it had been, that might've made things easier, but Lachie had returned from his father's that Monday. If she asked Alex to take Lachie this coming weekend as well—and heaven forbid from Thursday night to Monday morning—she'd never hear the end of it. Alex would grumble and groan at the request, and even if he did agree to take Lachie, there was an even chance he'd cancel at the last minute.

And asking Alex's parents to look after Lachie? Well, that wasn't an option. When Lucy had fallen pregnant and decided to have Lachie, Alex's father, Derick, had told everyone straight up that she could not count on him for support. At the time Lucy had assumed it was simply his way of trying to persuade Lucy not to go ahead with the pregnancy, but he had made good on his threat, and Alex's father was available for only very brief and occasional visits with Lachie. And even that contact came with snide comments from Derick about how Lucy had been so irresponsible to fall pregnant in the first place. It never seemed to occur to him that Alex may have played a part in Lachie's conception.

She'd have to ask her parents.

Or she could tell Marcus she couldn't go. Tell him it was absolutely impossible.

But she didn't want to do that. Marcus looked at her expectantly, waiting for her response. The crinkle crossed his brow, furrowed in confusion.

They can't believe I'm not jumping at this chance. I can't believe I'm not ecstatic at the chance to go to Fiji in the middle of winter. To leave rainy, miserable Sydney to visit rainforests and tropical reefs. To go swimming, snorkelling, to spend time with her devastatingly handsome boss. Who in their right mind would refuse an opportunity like that?

'We'll fly business class, of course. It'll be tiring but hopefully you'll be able to relax on the plane.'

Business class? They were trying to break her, weren't they?

'Can I have some time to think about it?' she asked.

'We need to let OZ know straight away. Is there something…?' He didn't finish the question, but this was her opening. Her opportunity to tell him why she'd love to go with him. More than anything. But why it was utterly impossible.

Yes, there is something. I have a five-year-old son I haven't told you about. I fell pregnant to my high school boyfriend. He's an indifferent father and his parents never miss an opportunity to tell me how much I've ruined their son's life by deciding to keep their grandchild. I don't know how I can ask my parents to look after him while I'm gone—they'd have to take Friday off work and they'd probably be late in on Monday after the drop-off. I'm also not sure how I can bear to travel overseas without him.

'Can I let you know in an hour?' she asked. 'There's just something I have to sort out.'

He stepped back from the desk and lifted his hands in the air, as though in surrender. 'Of course,' he said, his words and his tone contradicting his body language.

'Thank you, Marcus, and I'm sorry I just have to...' No, she *didn't* need to explain. She had said all she needed to say. Her explanation was perfectly reasonable. Lucy stood and left Marcus's office, without a further look at him and his slim-cut pants. Surely designed by someone who was attempting to encourage office romances and break the resolution of co-workers everywhere.

Lucy grabbed her phone from her desk and took the lift down to the ground floor. There was no way she could have this conversation anywhere in the office.

Out on the street it was windy, and the clouds looked like they were ready to burst, but she ducked into the nearest alleyway, passed a few smokers and found a place where an overhanging ledge provided some shelter. She pressed her mother's number.

Kate Spencer instantly agreed to look after Lachie, which didn't make Lucy feel any better at all.

'I'm so sorry, Mum, I just don't know what else to do.'

'Lucy, don't think anything of it. This is a once-in-a-lifetime opportunity—of course you have to go.'

'I'll ask Alex, but you know him.'

'No need to do that sweetheart. We can talk about it more tonight. Just go and tell your boss you'll go.'

Ten minutes later Lucy was windswept but back knocking on Marcus's door. He looked up from his screen and waved her in. Lucy closed his office door behind her.

'Thank you, Marcus, I'd love to come to Fiji with you.'

A cautious grin spread across Marcus's face.

'I'm glad to hear that, Lucy. Is everything okay?'

'Everything is wonderful, thank you, Marcus.'

'Lucy, I want it to be crystal clear that this trip is purely professional.'

'Of course… I mean, of course… I didn't.' She was stuttering and stammering like someone who had obviously considered the propriety and possibilities of two people who were pretty obviously attracted to one another spending the weekend in tropical, romantic surroundings…

'I only mean that I hope I haven't made you uncomfortable or made things difficult for you. This is a work trip, nothing more.'

'I know.'

'I just thought that perhaps you might have someone…that you might be seeing someone who might be concerned…'

'No, that is, not I'm not seeing anyone. I'm single.'

That tiny, innocuous phrase seemed to suck all the air from the room. Marcus froze. Lucy held her breath. That's what he thought she was worried about? That she had a boyfriend who might not like that she was going to tropical Fiji for a few days with her gorgeous boss?

He rubbed his thumb against the palm of his opposite hand. *He does that when he's nervous. Or embarrassed.* Something inside her twisted; that was a strange thing to know about someone.

He nodded. 'I'll get Tara to send you all the details. If you have any special dietary requirements or anything in particular you might need for this travel, please let her know.'

She nodded. She was pretty sure babysitter was not on the list of special requirements he had in mind.

'Marcus,' she began, 'do you have a moment?'

He looked perplexed, glanced at his screen and then back to her. This was it. She just had to do it. Just pull this Band-Aid off. What could possibly go wrong?

A loud ring from his phone made them both glance at it. When Marcus looked back up to Lucy, he said, 'Could you give me five minutes? I have to take this.'

Lucy shook her head quickly. 'No, no it's fine. Not important, I'll talk to Tara. Thank you very much again, Marcus,' she muttered as she scurried out of his office and closed his door behind her, fingers shaking. Sitting back at her desk, she tried, without much success, to steady her breath.

CHAPTER SIX

ONCE LACHIE WAS in bed, Kate Spencer put on the kettle and made Lucy tell her all about the trip.

'They liked our provisional pitch and we're going to present to the board in a month's time. That's amazing as it is—the trip was a complete surprise. The others are going to Bali.'

'So basically you're sightseeing with your hot boss for three days?'

'How do you know he's hot?'

'He is, isn't he?'

Lucy looked into her tea.

'Your father and I googled him when you got the job. He looks very handsome in the photos. Or is he not that good-looking in real life?'

Lucy didn't want to tell her that the photo didn't do him justice. In person, he was overwhelming.

'We'll be working,' was all Lucy said.

'Of course, of course. Just the two of you?'

'There's no need to smirk.'

Kate held up her palms. 'I'm not sure why we're even discussing this.'

'It's just so long. It's three days, two nights.'

'You've been away from Lachie before.'

'Yes, but I've never gone so far away.'

'Are you worried about the distance, or something else?'

'Mum,' she warned.

'Lucy, sweetheart, it a fantastic opportunity. A big trip away to work on a huge campaign! I'm so proud of you.'

Kate reached across the kitchen table and squeezed Lucy's hand. 'I never doubted you'd get here. And you haven't done it the easy way. I'm in awe of how hard you've worked and how much you've achieved. I won't let you miss out on this.'

'Thanks, Mum.' Lucy took her hand back and stood before she got teary like her mother. She took the empty mugs to the dishwasher.

'I bet you'll fly business class.'

Lucy nodded. 'That's what they said.'

'I've always wanted to fly business class.'

Lucy's chest felt tight. Her parents had always wanted to travel more. Downsize. But with Lucy and Lachie still living with them, they had never had the chance to sell the house or enjoy the leisure time they might have if Lucy had lived her life in the correct order.

'I'm sorry, Mum.'

'Sorry? What on earth for?'

'For…you know. If I… Lachie. You and Dad might have travelled more.'

'Lucy-Goosey don't be ridiculous. We've been over this I don't know how many times. We wouldn't give up Lachie for the all the business class travel in the world.'

Lucy's eyes began to sting. She believed her

mother, and yet it didn't assuage her worries altogether.

'Would you mind if I didn't ask Alex?'

'Of course not, but Lucy, he is Lachie's father.'

'I know, but I'm not sure it's worth it.'

Kate's brow creased. 'Worth what?'

'Worth hearing it all again.'

Kate didn't have to ask what Lucy meant. If she asked Alex to care for Lachie at any time other than their previously agreed dates she'd hear the resentment in Alex's tone. And while Alex would never come right out and say it, his father certainly would. *It was your choice to ruin your life. Don't expect us to do anything. Selfish, irresponsible, unable to fulfil your own responsibilities...*

'Alex asked you to look after Lachie last Friday night,' Kate said.

'But somehow that's different, isn't it?'

'I don't see how.'

'Because he's Alex and I'm me. It was my choice, so Lachie's my responsibility.'

'Lucy, darling, we all love him. We're all glad he's here.'

'You are. Derick Rankin isn't.'

'Derick is a grumpy old so-and-so.'

Lucy knew she was right, but that didn't make her feel any better.

Alex's parents had been against her keeping Lachie from the start. Lucy knew they were coming from a place of love for their son, but it still hurt, and it hurt Lachie too, which was worse. He was old enough now to see their behaviour and recognise that his paternal grandparents treated him very differently to his maternal grandparents.

'So Marcus doesn't have a problem with you having Lachie, does he?'

Lucy looked down again. The pattern on the tablecloth was fascinating.

'Oh, Lucy! You still haven't told him, have you?'

'I haven't had a chance.'

Kate snorted. 'It's not like you to be like that.'

'To lie?'

'I meant to be scared about something.'

'Mum, I'm scared of lots of things.'

'That may be so, but you're also the bravest person I know.'

Lucy knew what her mother was referring to—everyone referred to her decision to have and keep Lachie as 'brave' but that was only a euphemism for 'stupid'.

Lucy didn't feel brave at all.

That night, she stood in front of her open wardrobe and sighed deeply. Dressing for work each day was difficult enough, but dressing for business travel? Looking elegant, professional, and staying comfortable? Not to mention what she was going to wear once they got to Fiji. Sure, it wasn't the middle of summer, but Fiji was tropical. Humid.

And she had no idea what they'd be doing. 'Experiencing the Pacific like a tourist,' Marcus had said. But did that mean dressing like a tourist as well? Not when you were trying to maintain a professional facade because if you didn't, if you let yourself slip into thinking that the trip away was somehow fun, then you'd fall into all sorts of trouble.

No. It was business only. Professional. So why did it feel as though she was packing for a romantic weekend away?

In her lunchbreak the next day, Lucy ducked out of the office for a quick trip to the shops. The Sydney boutiques were hardly bursting with resort wear in July but she managed to find some casual yet neat blouses, from the leftover summer range. Fortunately, being out of season, these were also on sale. On the way to the change room she also spotted a light blue sundress that she added the pile. The blouses fitted well, and they were comfortable, yet not too casual. The dress, on the other hand, was also comfortable, but it dipped a bit too low down her cleavage to be described as professional. The sales assistant noticed her wavering and pointed out that it was also half-price and Lucy was late back for work so didn't argue.

Together with some shorts and pants in her

wardrobe, she figured she managed to pull together a look that could match whatever it was that Marcus was going to throw at her.

Except, perhaps, Marcus himself.

Friday morning was hard; they had an early flight from Sydney airport and Marcus had arranged for a car to pick her up just after six. As the car pulled up to the curb, Lucy held her son tight and tried to sound calm and relaxed so he wouldn't worry. She didn't want him to pick up on her anxiety.

But Lachie was fine.

In the end, Lucy had told Alex she was going away, only to let him know her movements. To her great surprise, he had offered to have Lachie for the day on Saturday. It was something at least.

'Dad's going to take me to the zoo. And we might see Nanna and Grandad too.'

At the mention of Alex's father, Lucy flinched. She could just imagine what he'd say: *Business trip to Fiji? Give me a break. Just an excuse to avoid her responsibilities.*

You're an irresponsible teenage mother...

Alex's father hadn't even met Lachie until he was three months old and never saw him, unless his wife, Alex's mother, was also there. Of all Lachie's grandparents, Derick Rankin was the one who had contributed the least, but if you'd asked him he'd say that the impact Lachie's arrival had had on his life had been nothing less than shattering.

'We'll video call every day. You can use Granny's phone to call me anytime.'

She'd miss him so much her chest would ache, but she knew that growing her career would be a good thing for Lachie in the end.

And Alex's father would just have to live with it.

CHAPTER SEVEN

SHE SAID SHE was single. But she still had to check something or arrange something or ask for someone's permission for her to go away on a work trip. Maybe she had a pet? A dog that needed feeding and walking? At least he'd taken his mother's advice and not said anything up-front to Lucy. His mother, as usual, was right. Lucy just had a life. He was relieved that his suspicions about a controlling partner had been wrong.

Though she still wasn't being entirely truthful with him.

Lucy sat across a low table from him now, in the business lounge at the airport, as they waited for their four-hour flight to Nadi.

OZ Airways had designed a full itinerary for them that would let them experience travel in all perspectives and budgets, though a glance at the itinerary showed most activities were at the luxury end of the travel spectrum. They would arrive in Fiji just before lunchtime and then travel straight to the hills and rainforest behind Nadi. Abseiling and zip-lining over the rainforest canopy and into some caves had been planned, and Marcus's mouth went a little dry just thinking about it, but it was all part of what OZ called 'experiencing the best tropical Fiji had to offer.'

Marcus went rock climbing occasionally, so how hard could abseiling be? It was only going down, not climbing up, after all.

This evening they would return to Denarau Island, near Nadi, where they would stay for a night at an exclusive resort before a trip out to one of the most exclusive island resorts. Tara had winked at him as she'd handed him a printed version of the itinerary.

He knew how it looked, going away with a beautiful young woman on a two-night full luxury travel experience. But he was professional, had always been so, and Marcus knew that Tara and Daphne's ribbing was only friendly. Besides, his potential client was insisting they go.

Lucy sipped her coffee and looked around the lounge curiously. Looking everywhere but at him. She seemed jumpy from the moment they had met in the arrivals hall. She was apprehensive about something.

He wished he knew what was going on behind those beautiful brown eyes, what made her tick.

A family sat at the group of armchairs next to them. The kids were young, Marcus didn't have much experience with kids so couldn't possibly guess how old they were, but they were at the ages were they were climbing over the chairs and making a nuisance of themselves.

One of the boys rolled over the back of the armchairs and slipped, almost landing on Lucy.

Marcus sighed. The mother reprimanded her son and then turned to Lucy and apologised.

'It's fine, really,' Lucy insisted.

When it happened again, the parents picked up their kids and relocated to a table at the back of the lounge and away from the others.

'Don't move on our account,' Lucy said, but the parents shook their heads.

'They shouldn't travel if they can't control their children,' Marcus said.

Lucy scoffed. 'That's a bit harsh. Even the best parents can't control their children all the time. Besides, we have no idea why they're travelling. It may not be a holiday.' As reprimands went, it was soft but effective.

He felt his lips tug into a grin, despite himself. 'You're right.' There were all kinds of reasons that family might have to be travelling with young children, and the parents, now that he came to think about it, didn't seem terribly happy to be there. If anything, they looked stressed and upset. 'I don't know any kids. I don't understand the attraction.'

Lucy wrinkled her nose. It was a beautiful nose and real shame to screw it up like she did.

'You don't think you'll ever have any?'

Many women had asked him that question over the years. Usually with their hand stroking his forearm, looking up at him with expectant eyes. Lucy sat where she was, head cocked to one side as though she'd just asked him if he wanted another coffee.

He shook his head. 'I know what you're about to say, "You'll change your mind one day." Well, I haven't and I won't.'

Lucy shrugged and asked casually, 'Why not, if you don't mind me asking?'

She sat across from him, her arms crossed on the table she leaned across. An empty coffee cup and half-eaten breakfast in front of her. She was dressed in loose blue pants and a dusty pink blouse that matched the colour of her lips perfectly. He wondered if it was on purpose or if she had been drawn to the pink because it was simply in a beautiful colour. Suddenly this was not work Lucy who had secrets she guarded like her life depended on it. This was like having coffee with a friend. And unlike the other women who had asked him whether he wanted to have children, she wasn't touching his knee, as if to persuade him to the contrary.

For moment he considered telling her about Joel. And his father. Then he remembered Lucy wasn't a friend or a date. She was a colleague and it wasn't appropriate for him to be telling her about his brother and the event that had changed his life irrevocably. He'd only ever told a handful of people the real story, and those were his oldest school friends, who had known Joel anyway.

It wasn't so much a matter of telling them what had happened, but filling in the blanks.

He didn't tell women he dated. He didn't even tell his newer friends, but he thought about telling Lucy.

'This is a message for passengers travelling to Nadi on Flight OZ456. This flight is now boarding. Please make your way to Gate Lounge C.'

'That's us,' Lucy said, standing and picking up her bag.

They were collected at the airport by their guide, Joe. '*Bula*—welcome to Fiji. I will drop you at your tour and take your bags to the resort,' he told them.

'So we won't be staying at the Nadi backpackers' hostel?' Lucy grinned and her entire face lit up.

He couldn't help but smile back. He smiled a lot with Lucy. He liked how it felt, and he liked the way the muscles in his face felt different, how his chest and shoulders felt lighter.

'We can if you want. I'll cancel the booking at the Beach Pavilion on Denarau.'

Lucy tilted her head and placed her finger to her chin in faux contemplation. 'No, I wouldn't like to make a fuss. And OZ went to all that trouble.'

They drove out of the airport, in the direction of the hills in the distance. Mist clung to the deep green walls of the mountains. He breathed in deeply, the humid air instantly soothing his winter-dry Sydney skin. Next to him, Lucy had taken off her jacket and he noticed the smooth white skin of her forearms. She titled her head back, as though to catch more of the sun and the warm tropical air. She closed her eyes and sighed, either forgetting he was there next to her or not caring that he was. Something stirred deep inside him. He turned back to the road in front of him just in time to make the next turn safely.

Lucy jerked upright. 'So where are off to? You haven't even given me an itinerary. Is the Magical Mystery Tour the client's idea too?'

'We're staying tonight on Denarau, as you know.' Denarau was a small island, not far from Nadi, connected to the mainland by a bridge, and populated with luxurious resorts. 'But first, we're booked in for a trip into the hills and into the rainforest.'

They boarded a bus with open windows and several other groups travelling into the hills. As it wound its way up the steep escarpment, the world next to him dipped away, leaving only uninterrupted views back towards Nadi and the ocean. Marcus scanned the cabin. He and Lucy were the only people not over seventy, under seven or the parents of passengers under seven.

The children on the bus made the ones at the airport this morning look like angels. They were

'I am,' Marcus said quickly and strongly. If this Semesa was actually a cowboy operator and not the reputable operator Tara had told him about, then Marcus would be the one to get smashed against the rock, not Lucy. Lucy's eyes flickered but Marcus turned.

His forearms suddenly didn't feel strong enough to hold a pen, let along his own weight; they were shaky and strange. Memories of Joel and that terrible day flooded his thoughts. He stood at the cliff edge, unable to move. What was he going to do? He couldn't go down—he could hardly move.

'Marcus? Are you all right?'

Lucy's voice jolted him back to the present and he took a deep breath. Blocking out all thoughts about Joel and that horrible day, he listened to Semesa's encouraging words and eased himself over the edge, looking to the next rock and never the drop below. There was enough to concentrate on, making his way carefully over the rocks, looking for safe spaces to place his feet, searching for the next landing point. He caught glimpses of the lush green rainforest, allowed himself to notice the deep perfect blue of the sky and the way the birdsong surrounded them and eventually relaxed into the motion and stopped to glance around and take in the gushing water, the mist that floated through the gorge. And then before he was ready, it was over and he was safely on the ground next to Semesa's assistant. His limbs were still shaky, not with fear but with exhilaration.

He landed, so glad he hadn't died and that no one would have to explain to his mother that her second son had perished in an accident.

Minutes later, Lucy was beside him, her face flushed and eyes bright. She grabbed his arm. 'Wasn't that amazing?'

Marcus could only nod in agreement.

Semesa smiled at her and said, 'If you loved that, you're going to love the zip-lining.'

Marcus wanted to stay there, standing on the smooth grey rocks and drink in Lucy's enthusiasm. But he had four zip-lines and one more descent to get through.

He didn't think he'd seen Lucy so carefree. Not that he'd known her long or could claim to know her well, but seeing her, bouncing her heels, admiring the spectacular scenery, she seemed lighter, less burdened than she did in Sydney. In the office she seemed on alert, watching over her shoulder. Now, despite the fact her life was literally hanging by a rope, she was living entirely in the moment.

Lucy was giddy with adrenaline. There was nothing in the world she couldn't do. She was smiling so hard her cheeks hurt. She knew she probably looked ridiculous. Manic even. But she didn't care. The scenic location, the sun, the sensation of gliding over treetops and waterfalls, all of it. Her life back in Sydney seemed so distant. She had hoped that starting at Oracle would give her a chance to live a different life, but this was another level completely. She wasn't Lachie's mum. Or her parents' daughter. Or Alex's ex. For the first time in as long as she could remember, she was just Lucy.

They tackled one more cliff and some ziplines before they met the bus to take them back to their hotel. Marcus was uncharacteristically quiet, though that could just have been because he couldn't get a word in past Lucy and her enthusiastic babbling. She knew she was going on and on about how great it was but she couldn't stop herself. She felt so happy she didn't even care if Marcus thought she sounded like a goose.

'Did you have a good time?' she asked.

'It was great,' he replied, though his tone was not as passionate as Lucy's. And maybe that was appropriate; it was a business trip after all. They were technically working.

Never mind. She would show him she could enjoy herself and still stay focused on the task at hand as he was.

Marcus's heart caught in his throat when the bus emerged from the dense rainforest to see the spectacular view of the ocean spread our beneath them. The dense jungle spread all the way to the edge of the pristine white beach and the blue water. The sun was close to setting and the sky was every shade of pink. The scene looked like it had been painted. It looked like a place from his dreams; it was one of the most beautiful sights he'd seen in his life.

Almost as beautiful as Lucy, he thought and instantly batted the thought away.

Lucy turned to look at him, the smile on her face as dazzling as the turquoise water. 'Isn't it just about the most beautiful place you've ever seen?'

Marcus could only nod, for he had a view of the beach and Lucy's beaming face.

'It's just...' Lucy shook her head, speechless. 'I can't explain it—there is almost something magical about this place.'

Marcus couldn't agree more.

As the bus nudged its way down the mountain, Lucy's thigh gently bumped against his, making Marcus's leg tingle.

'Is it what you were expecting?' he asked to distract himself form the sensation.

'Yes... No, it was so much more. I learnt so much but it was also...' She sighed, lost for words.

'Fun?'

Her smile lit up her face. 'So much fun. I wish I'd got my camera out fast enough to catch the look on your face when you took that last zip-line.

'It is such a beautiful place. I almost feel calm.' His eyes were firmly on the road, checking the progress of the bus, but he felt Lucy's intense gaze on his left cheek. Singing, burning, marking him.

'You don't often, do you? Feel calm?' she asked.

He felt in control, busy, but not calm. He shook his head.

'Why?'

'I'm not anxious, but I have things to do.'

'Like what? Tell me.'

The light had nearly faded and the bus had nearly finished its descent down the mountain, so he allowed himself to take his eyes from the road and relax. He found it was easy to open up to her in the dark, as they weaved through the forest, back to the hotel. 'Oracle is my life. It is a success, but it hasn't been easy. It has taken every ounce of energy I've had over the past decade.'

Quite without meaning to, he told her about starting up Oracle, his first fumbling attempts to bring in business, the failures, the successes. Lucy listened attentively. After the day they had spent together, it was natural to open up to her, and there was something intoxicating about bumping along, in the warm tropical night, that made him want to tell her everything. Before he knew it, they were pulling into the resort.

CHAPTER EIGHT

IT WAS DARK when the bus delivered them to the valet parking section of the hotel. Several white pavilions were nestled amongst lush green gardens, sparking pools and streams. They were greeted enthusiastically by the hotel staff with, '*Ni sa bula!* Welcome to the Beach Pavilion.'

'Why don't we freshen up before heading to dinner?' Marcus suggested. 'We have a booking at eight.'

'Great.' That would give her time to call Lachie and have a few moments' respite from Marcus's company. While she had had a wonderful day, she was becoming too comfortable around him, too relaxed. He was beginning to feel too much like a friend and not enough like a boss. And where Marcus was concerned, she knew for the sake of self-preservation that barriers and boundaries were important. Marcus was the sort of man she could easily fall for. Not that she had—no, she was being very careful to remind herself of all the reasons why Marcus Hawke was off-limits, but sometimes your heart didn't listen to your head. Particularly when your body was whispering traitorous things such as *Check out those arms. Look at the way the muscles in his backside flex when he's rappelling down the cliff.* Parts of her clenched that hadn't clenched in years when she remembered the sight of Marcus's muscular thighs as he descended the cliff...

She purposefully replaced that memory with the one of his reaction to the children at the airport lounge and Marcus's insistence that he didn't want children, and in that way she reassured herself that her heart was safe from being ensnared by Marcus. He might be a brilliant creator, a great boss. Even a good man. But Lucy could never see herself with a man who didn't adore children. She'd already made that mistake.

Her suite was spectacular; furnished tastefully with white linens, comfortable couches and enormous vases overflowing with tropical flowers. Her private balcony had a view over a grove of palm trees and the ocean beyond. Lucy had to suppress all the thoughts telling herself she didn't belong here.

Lachie was happy to hear from her, though after a quick hello his attention wavered and he wanted to get back to his LEGO. Kate assured Lucy that he had had a good day at school, that they were all fine and that she should go back to enjoying herself.

'Are you managing to keep your hands off that gorgeous boss of yours?' she asked.

'Mum!' Lucy whispered, as though the hotel walls were paper-thin and Marcus may have overheard. 'Of course. This is a work trip.'

'How's the work going then?'

'Well,' Lucy lied. They had talked about lots of things today, the beauty of the scenery, the spectacular sights, but not the campaign. Dinner. They would talk about it at dinner. Brainstorm ideas then.

Marcus was waiting for her outside the foyer after she'd changed. She wore another pair of loose pants, her new floral blouse. Smart casual. Definitely not an outfit for a date. Because this wasn't a date. Even though Marcus turned and looked at her expectantly and smiled when she approached.

He'd changed too, into tan pants and a white shirt with the top buttons undone. She could have drooled, he looked so edible.

We should put him in the commercial. Plenty of tourists would be sure to want a board a plane if there was a possibility of meeting him at the other end.

His eyes darted quickly up and down her figure and she felt herself being appraised, but also admired. Her skin warmed. Tropical heat plus admiring stares equalled a very discombobulated Lucy.

'We should brainstorm ideas about the campaign,' she blurted. She had to focus on the pitch and not the way the Marcus's evening stubble looked so appealing against his crisp white shirt.

Marcus cleared his throat. 'Yes, definitely, we

should.' He motioned for her to begin walking down the long, tree-lined path to the restaurant. Lucy wrinkled her nose as the smell accosted her nostrils. It was unfamiliar, pungent. Not bad, but distinctive.

'What is that?' she asked.

'Guano.'

'Is that…?'

'Bat poop, yes. Too much?'

'No, it's not terrible, but definitely tropical. But let's not mention it in the campaign.'

Marcus laughed. 'What should we mention?'

Lucy sighed. The campaign should mention the fact that travelling can help you forget the life you've left behind. How it can make you imagine a different, impossible life where you aren't here on a business trip but here on holiday. Or a honeymoon.

'We could say how good warm air feels on your skin.' Lucy opened her arms wide to take full advantage of the humid air on her sun-deprived winter skin. She may have made a low moaning noise. Marcus gave her a funny look and her skin turned from pleasantly warm to burning.

She had to stop getting all the sexy feelings about the tropical air in front of her boss.

Marcus stopped outside a restaurant. Lucy knew without even looking at the menu that this was the sort of place she would never go unless someone else was picking up the cheque.

They were shown to a table on the balcony, overlooking the lagoon and the ocean beyond. Lights from the restaurant reflected in the calm waters.

'It's beautiful,' Lucy said. 'So calm.'

'It looks that way, but there are venomous sea snakes, blue-ringed octopi and even saltwater crocs just beneath the surface.'

'Really?' Lucy found it hard to believe; the water surrounding them looked so calm and beautiful.

'I looked it up,' he replied with a shrug.

They locked eyes and he held her gaze. His eyes, which had looked like the colour of a tropical lagoon earlier that day, were now the colour of midnight. Her gut tightened. And not from smelling the delicious aromas emanating from the kitchen, but from the look in the eyes of the man sitting across from her. Hunger.

There was danger below the surface of the water. There was danger below the surface of this dinner. Sea snakes. Crocodiles.

She wished he wouldn't look at her like that, yet craved it at the same time. In her experience, men tended not to look at women with that same intensity when they were attached to a small child. It was intoxicating, for once, to be on the receiving end of a look like that, and surely she was safe. Surely he understood he was her boss, and she was the employee. They could look, just not touch.

They were presented with a five-course degustation with oysters, seared scallops, prawns, duck breast and mango soufflé with matching wine for each course.

Lucy's parents enjoyed good wine and had taught her to differentiate a well-made wine from a badly constructed one, but she was unaccustomed to the richness of the meal and the wine.

By the third course her stomach was stretched. She looked at her dessert wondering how she would manage it.

'Is everything okay?' Marcus asked, concerned.

'It's more than okay. I'm just not used to eating so much. It's amazing, but… I don't go to places like this very often.'

'Really? A gorgeous single woman like you? I bet you have invites like this every day.'

Oh, no, this was crocodile territory. She shook her head and batted away his comment, or was it a compliment? 'No, not really,' she replied. There hadn't been anyone since Alex. Not that she could tell Marcus that.

Marcus gave her a quizzical look. 'This is the most exclusive restaurant on Denarau, I thought if we experienced it, we might get into the mood.'

Into the mood?

'For what?' she asked, not able to disguise the look of shock on her face. Making love? Romance? The crocodiles were definitely awake and on the move.

'To develop ideas for the pitch.'

'Of course,' Lucy scoffed. 'If we're pitching to honeymooners.'

'And why wouldn't we? Honeymooners are one of the biggest markets to Fiji.'

'Oh, right, okay. Of course. It's just that when I think of the audience I imagine the tourists we saw on the bus. The retirees, the families.'

'We'll think about them too. But for now, let's think about honeymooners. What would we say to lure them here?'

Lucy's head spun. All the wine and rich food. This luxury travel thing was great, until your boss asked you a question like that and the world started spinning around you. She was exhausted and tipsy. Marcus was hard enough to handle when she was fully alert and caffeinated, let alone in the state she was now. One more smile from him and goodness knows what she'd say to him. Do to him.

'Well, it's beautiful.'

'Obviously.'

'And to be quite honest, my life in Sydney seems so far away. I feel like a different person.'

Marcus stared at her across the table, studying her so hard she felt naked.

'But that's probably not what you want to tell honeymooners.' He smiled and she felt her face grow even hotter.

'No, but the idea of escape, finding yourself, that's good too, isn't it? That would capture the overworked, sun-deprived market. Getting away from it all, that sort of thing?'

'Yes, it would. But what about honeymooners? What would we want them to know about this place?'

He was impossible. Was he meaning to taunt her? Was he trying to flirt, or was this a genuine work-related question? She couldn't tell anymore.

Lucy hadn't had a lover since Alex. At first she'd had no time, because Lachie had needed so much of her. Then she lacked desire; she had other things to focus on. Then logistics blocked her way. She'd downloaded a dating app and chatted to a few men, but each time they had suggested meeting she'd found an excuse to decline. But now, sitting across from Marcus, in a decidedly date-like situation, she regretted not going on at least a few dates. To stay in practice. To learn how to deal with the rush of emotions currently tumbling through her body.

'I've never been on a honeymoon, so I'm not really sure,' she said.

He raised just one of his dark eye-framing brows. 'Not sure about romance? Love?'

She shook her head. She had to regain control of the conversation. And her heart rate. 'What about you?'

The grin on his face tightened. 'I've never been on a honeymoon either.'

'Then I guess neither of us are qualified to

say what a honeymooner wants in a holiday.' She crossed her arms, hoping the conversation was over.

'Yes, but we're not retirees or parents either, and we still have to imagine what they are looking for as well. We have to appeal to a broader audience than just overworked young professionals.'

Lucy swallowed, unable to meet Marcus's eye. 'I guess I'd tell a honeymooner that this is just the sort of place for falling in love.'

'We should probably assume the honeymooners are already in love,' he teased.

'Falling in love again? It's not the sort of place where you would fall out of love.'

Marcus laughed. 'No, I guess it isn't.' He pushed his mango soufflé around his plate. 'Fall in love,' he murmured. 'Fall backwards off a cliff.' He looked up and Lucy didn't look away fast enough to avoid his gaze.

There was a vulnerability in it; he was referring to the way he had paused so long at the top of the cliff this afternoon she thought he was going to chicken out of it. He looked at her as though he were considering mentioning it, explain it. Then, just when she thought he was going to open up about something, he shook his head as though remembering where he was. 'Fall in love? Fall down under?'

Lucy laughed.

'Okay, maybe not.' Marcus laughed too.

'Anyway.' She wanted to change the subject to something far removed from honeymoons or lovers. She glanced around at the beautiful location, the lights sparkling on the calm lagoon, felt the still, tropical air on her dry winter skin. 'So, is this unusual for you, or just an everyday week in the life of the director of a creative agency?'

'Oh, you know. It was Tahiti last month, Paris the month before last.'

Lucy's mouth dropped.

'No.' He shook his head. 'This is a serious perk.'

For the briefest of seconds his expression hardened. As though he'd remembered something he'd rather forget.

'I know it would be a massive deal for Oracle. But it's more than that, isn't it?' she said.

He didn't answer.

'It feels almost…personal,' she prompted, and when his eyes narrowed she realised she'd made a mistake. She pressed her lips together. She'd done it again. Brought up the personal when she was trying her hardest to keep things professional.

Marcus nodded. 'In a way, it is. I've always wanted to do the big campaigns.'

'Like the big corporates?'

'No, not exactly. The information campaigns. The safety campaigns, the government accounts.'

'You want to change people's behaviour?'

'Yes, I do,' he said and nodded.

All advertising was changing behaviour in some

way, but Marcus didn't just want to sell stuff. He wanted to change people's attitudes. It was refreshing, but the expression on his face was strangely serious. She wanted to ask more, but his eyes warned her not to probe.

'What about you?' he asked. *Way to change the subject, Marcus.* 'What drew you to design?'

She didn't know how to answer his question any way other than with absolute honesty. 'It was the one thing I was good at.'

'I find that very hard to believe.'

I flunked out of high school.

'I'm not very academic.'

He looked at her under a furrowed brow. 'Your university marks were excellent.'

She looked down. 'Thank you. But I had a hard time at high school. My art results were good and the university looked at those when they offered me a place.' She had passed her final year on the second attempt, but her results in the 'serious' subjects were way below what everyone would have expected of her. If she hadn't had Lachie. The university had a special entrance program for students with extenuating life circumstances where they looked beyond just the academic results and to the person's other achievements.

They had offered her a place and she hadn't let them down.

Thankfully, he didn't enquire further. The cheque arrived as if the waitstaff could sense this conversation had just run its course.

They paused in the vast lobby of the hotel. The tiredness hit her. This morning seemed so distant, like it was three days ago not just this morning. Her thoughts were full, but annoyingly, only of Marcus. And as he stood there, facing her, also in silence, she wondered what he was waiting for.

If you weren't colleagues, if this was a date, this would be the part where you kiss.

Lucy shook herself. She'd drunk just enough wine, was feeling just happy and safe enough that if she didn't get out of there soon, she might persuade herself that standing on her toes and leaning to Marcus and his nine-o'clock shadow and heavy-lidded eyes would not be a completely terrible idea.

She had to get some sleep and tomorrow she would fill her mind with things that weren't about Marcus.

'Thank you for dinner,' she said.

'My pleasure.'

Was it her imagination or was his voice thicker? Her own throat was tight and dry and she had only a sliver of self-control remaining to say, 'See you tomorrow.' Then she turned and headed in the direction she hoped her room was in.

CHAPTER NINE

LUCY SLEPT BETTER than she'd expected to. The sound of the ocean had rocked her to sleep and kept her lulled in comfort, free from yesterday's roller-coaster of emotions regarding Marcus. She woke early and refreshed. It was just after six and the sky was lightening. She had agreed to meet Marcus for breakfast at eight so calculated she had time to explore and possibly a swim before that. Judging by the sounds of gently lapping waves, she wasn't far from the beach. If not the beach, the hotel was so luxurious there would be several swimming pools to choose from. She slipped on her red one-piece, wrapped a floral sarong around her waist and went to explore.

She was right; the hotel sat alongside the ocean and her villa was one of the closest to the beach. A few early-morning joggers and walkers were making the most of the perfect conditions, and she wondered if the water would be warm enough to dip a toe into. The tropical ocean was relatively calm and a few other swimmers were in the water, so she figured it would be safe. Despite Marcus's warnings the day before about sea snakes and crocodiles, she slipped off her sarong and laid it with her towel.

As she strolled to the water's edge, her throat

closed over. It was Marcus. Emerging from the ocean, naked except for a small pair of tight black shorts, dripping wet. Like Colin Firth emerging from the lake. Only with fewer clothes.

Marcus also stopped and his dropped jaw mirrored hers. For a moment they stared silently at one another, eyes darting up and down and then away into the distance.

'Did you sleep well?' he asked.

Momentarily thrown by his mundane question when the only expression that was forming in her mind was *Wow, what a chest*, Lucy hesitated. 'Um, yes, well. And you?'

'Very well. I think this ocean air agrees with me.'

'Me too.'

Marcus stepped towards her and Lucy instinctively stepped back. Marcus furrowed his brow. He stepped closer and she jumped back again.

'My towel.' He nodded to the hotel-issue beach towel that lay only metres from Lucy's toes. They were only feet away from one another, close enough that Lucy could see the individual drops of salt water sliding over his perfect olive skin, pooling in the dip of his collarbone and accentuating the definition in his abs. A slight smattering of hair covered his chest, trailing down to...

Look up, Lucy! For goodness' sake, what are trying to do to yourself?

She was suddenly very aware of her own muscles. All of her body, her skin, and especially the sensitive parts. Her breasts, her nipples, where they rubbed against the fabric of her swimsuit and especially, especially between her legs. Sensations she hadn't felt in years.

He reached past her and picked up his towel, and Lucy was treated the spectacle of his muscles moving underneath his skin as he moved and stretched. He began to towel himself dry and she looked away.

Even if Marcus was attracted to her, she couldn't bring him into Lachie's life. Anyone she brought home had to be special and willing to go the distance. It was bad enough that she and Alex hadn't been able to make things work. And then there were all the women Alex had dated while he'd been studying, a new one every year. Lucy had to give Lachie stability. She couldn't bring home just anyone. Especially not a workaholic who had made his feelings regarding children clear.

'How was the water?' she asked.

Marcus dragged the towel across his wet hair and regarded her for a long moment before replying, 'Beautiful.'

Lucy's skin began to burn. She nodded. 'Well, I'd better get in,' she said before she hurried to the ocean. She hoped it was cold. She needed to cool down. And fast.

* * *

Over a breakfast table laid with fresh tropical fruits and steaming hot coffee, Marcus opened his laptop and considered some proposals made by Liam and Daphne. They were good, but reservation still lurked within him. Were any of them good enough?

Lucy joined him after her swim, and his breath caught in his throat. She was considerably more attired than she had been at the beach, wearing loose pants with a happy floral pattern and a yellow blouse. She looked bright, lovely and impossibly pretty.

'Good morning,' she said brightly as she sat.

'Good morning.' So neither of them was going to mention the encounter on the beach. Which was probably just as well.

'How is everything?' she asked, nodding to his laptop.

'Fine. I'm looking at some material from Daphne and Liam.'

'Great,' she said.

Though it wasn't. And it was all Marcus's fault. If he hadn't been so distracted by other things: worrying about the abseiling, thinking about Lucy. If he concentrated on work, then there would be very little time left over for him and Lucy to be looking at each other over half-burnt candles talking about honeymoons and falling in love and stupid things like that.

Last night had been wonderful. Yesterday had been wonderful. If they spent another evening drinking, looking at each other across a candlelit table, then he might start to forget his resolve. He might start to feel more than he already had. More than he wanted to. More than he should. Especially since it was clear Lucy was still keeping her cards close to her chest. He'd had such a good day, loved that he'd been able to spend every moment of it with Lucy. He'd thought she was opening up to him, but like the mug he was, he was the one who had been doing all the sharing.

But then, why did he care? She was keeping a professional distance and, really, wasn't that the smart thing to do all around? It was just as well she wasn't opening up to him. His life was hard enough at the moment without complicating it with an office romance. He liked Lucy; he *really* liked her. But she was his employee. And a good employee. Possibly a great one. She was an asset that Oracle Creative wouldn't want to lose. That he didn't want to lose.

And the fact that he was attracted to her? That the skin on his chest and neck prickled when he caught sight of her, her soft brown hair and big honey eyes…well, that could be managed. It wouldn't be the most difficult thing he'd had to overcome in his life. When lined up alongside

the other challenges he'd faced, resisting Lucy
Spencer should be a doddle. He would have to
admire from a distance. A little sexual tension in
the office never hurt anyone. In fact, he'd sometimes seen it inspire others to worker longer,
harder. If this bit of tension between him and
Lucy prompted them both to work harder, then
how could that be a bad thing? And that's all it
was: a bit of tension. Probably because he hadn't
had the time to date anyone recently. That was
all it was. Nothing more.

He speared his fruit with a fork and concentrated on his breakfast and laptop.

CHAPTER TEN

A HELICOPTER! Just wait until she told Lachie. She took out her phone and snapped a quick photo.

When Marcus saw the tiny helicopter, the only aircraft on the runway, he stopped mid-stride. Lucy watched him with confusion. Her chest clenched. Marcus had given the same sort of pause the day before as he'd approached the cliff before abseiling. He'd stopped, stiffened, almost but not quite recoiled. He'd given away more than he'd intended to. A fear of heights? A fear of danger? After a deep breath and a small, almost imperceptible straightening of his spine, he continued walking towards the helicopter and held out his hand to let Lucy board first.

The helicopter rattled and shook as its blades started up. She put on the headset and couldn't hold back a smile, getting her phone out again for a quick selfie.

Unlike a plane, there wasn't much between herself and the stomach-flipping drop below.

She felt safe. She knew instinctively Marcus would never put her in any danger.

Her stomach dropped as the helicopter left the ground. The noise was immense and the vibrations powerful. Unlike on a plane, the clouds didn't quickly block their view of the earth below.

To the contrary, the pilot flew low enough to be sure they could see the magnificent sights beneath them. Colourful, bustling Nadi, which receded into the distance as they made their way up the coast; the lush verdant green of the island on one side; and to the other, the ocean, dotted with coral reefs and small sandy islands. The ocean sparkled like an exquisite jewel. Lucy couldn't stop oohing and aahing.

Next to her Marcus was silent and still. He was trying to keep a neutral expression, but Lucy could still see the muscles in his jaw clenched. His hand gripped the armrest between them. Lucy placed her hand on top of his.

He was nervous.

It was a highly presumptuous gesture. Inappropriate for junior employee and CEO, but somehow their relationship had moved beyond that. Maybe on the beach this morning. Maybe even long before that.

His eyes flashed at her briefly, and he attempted a smile. But Lucy saw through the attempt. She had to distract him with conversation.

'So what is on the agenda today? More abseiling? You've been very cagey about the itinerary. And why is that, by the way?'

'I want to surprise you, I guess.'

His blue eyes met hers and her stomach dropped too. Or that might have been the sharp turn the pilot took to loop the helicopter over the rainforest. Green spread out beneath them like a luxurious lawn, then the helicopter dipped again and swung out over the ocean, where they had perfect views of the emerald sea. Lucy gasped. The water was the most magnificent shades of blue and green she had seen—bluer, greener, brighter than she could have imagined.

'You do you surprise me, Marcus. Every day,' she said softly and squeezed his hand. She kept her hand rested on his.

'You should enjoy the view. Don't let my silly phobia keep you from enjoying the view.'

Phobia. He'd admitted it. She squeezed his hand again.

She liked that he trusted her enough to be vulnerable with her. Not completely vulnerable, it was true, but he'd acknowledged that he felt uncomfortable, rather than bluffing his way through it with fake bravado. She was touched, sensing he didn't tend to open up to anyone. He had a reputation as a fearless executive to uphold.

The water was so clear you could see the coral and the sandy ocean floor.

'I never knew it could be like this,' she said.

Marcus glanced past her, to the azure lagoon shimmering below. The islands were emerald green with patches of white.

'It's spectacular, isn't it?'

They arrived shortly afterwards at the Angel Isle Resort. The island where it was located was surrounded by a smattering of smaller, private islands and coral cays.

Once they were on the ground, Lucy turned on her phone. No signal. She sighed. She knew the hotel had a line so she could call home and she was contactable in case of an emergency, but she liked the idea of her mother being able to call her directly.

Nothing's going to happen...

Lachie was safe with her parents and would have a visit with Alex today. Everything was going to be fine. Lucy got out of the helicopter behind Marcus, who bounced down the stairs like he was a new man.

The Angel Isle Resort was the only business on the island, one of the most exclusive in Fiji.

They were directed to a small open-aired buggy which drove them and their luggage up a small hill to the resort itself. It was ridiculously beautiful. The view from the front of the lobby almost didn't look real; the colours so vibrant, it looked as though they had been overlaid with a high saturation filter.

'OZ have put together a detailed plan for you and Ms Spencer,' the receptionist at the front desk told Marcus. 'Snorkelling, stand-up paddleboarding, kayaking.' That sounded like a lot of activities with them only half-dressed. She remembered the encounter on the beach at Denarau where they were both in their swimmers. She remembered the sizzle in her belly and the look on his face. Desire mixed with pain.

Stand-up paddleboarding and kayaking might be okay. Snorkelling, however, could be risky.

'You're booked into the villa.' She passed Marcus one key card. Lucy waited for hers, but it didn't come.

'One room?' Lucy choked. It must be a mistake.

The woman laughed. 'One villa, many rooms. It's our most luxurious, with two master-sized bedrooms, large lounge, indoor and outdoor dining areas, a plunge pool and a valet service.' The woman's eyes twinkled.

'I suppose that will be suitable,' Lucy joked.

When Marcus turned and headed back to the buggy, the receptionist whispered to Lucy. 'I wouldn't mind having to share a single bunk with him.' She winked and Lucy's face burnt.

They were driven up the small hill to where their private villa sat on one of the highest points of the island. Climbing out of the buggy, she saw they had one-eighty-degree views of the island and the pristine ocean. 'Not every tourist is going to be able to afford an experience like this,' Lucy sighed.

'That's true. But we're also in the aspiration business.'

She nodded. 'Honestly, I don't think it would

matter where you are on this island—it's all spectacular.'

They explored the villa. Lucy headed in one direction, Marcus in the other.

The room she entered would probably technically have been called a bedroom, and it contained the biggest bed she'd ever seen. Wider than it was long. There was also a couch and armchairs which faced out onto a balcony, which in turn faced out into the treetops and the ocean beyond. Two doors led off the room, the first a walk-in closet. She'd brought a small suitcase only, could fill a few paltry drawers, barely making a dent in a closet bigger than the one she'd left at home. The other door led to a bathroom. A laugh bubbled up in her throat.

The bathroom had two sinks, and a bench bigger than her desk at work. A free-standing bathtub sat alongside the floor-to-ceiling window and overlooked the rainforest.

'What's so funny?' Marcus asked from the bedroom door and she jumped.

'Nothing. I mean, it's just…this.' Lucy spread her arms.

'It was presumptuous of them to put us in the same villa.'

'That's not what I meant and it's fine. Really.' She hadn't meant to sound so affronted when she found out they were in the same villa. She hadn't expected it to be so large. She felt awkward enough staying in such luxury as it was. 'One villa, many rooms. Besides, I suspect this is one of the most luxurious hotel suites in the South Pacific.'

'I think you might be right.'

'What's your room like?'

Marcus raised an eyebrow and grinned.

Watch out for the crocodiles, Lucy.

'Are you happy with it, or would you prefer this one?'

She asked out of politeness but Marcus grinned again.

'It is identical to this, but I'd be happy to swap if you prefer the view from the other.' He glanced past her to the bathroom with the exposed bathtub. Not for the first time that day Lucy's skin felt warm. It was the tropics, but this heating up whenever he looked at her was getting ridiculous.

'Anyway, OZ has us on a schedule. After a bit of paddleboarding and kayaking, we're booked in for a boat trip to the outer reef to go snorkelling.'

Snorkelling. Heaven help her and her last shred of self-control.

Their guide, Ela, met them at the beach to get them gear for the snorkelling trip. She offered them proper-fitting masks, snorkels and flippers. 'Due to the warm waters, the box jellyfish can be found at all times of the year now. We recommend you put these on.' She held up whole bodysuits. Thinner than a wetsuit, more like a full-body leotard. 'They also provide sun protection.'

Lucy grabbed the offered suit. It might look unattractive, but at least they wouldn't be looking at each other's skin.

'Feel free to change in one of the beach houses.' Ela directed them to the row of small but colourful huts on the edge of the beach. Once Lucy had the suit on, she looked at herself with a mixture of dismay and relief. On one hand, Marcus wouldn't be seeing her in a one-piece. On the other, she was wearing a bright blue full-body swimsuit.

She exited the hut, looking at the ground. When she finally met Marcus's eye, he was smirking.

'Just say it.'

'What?'

'I look like a Smurf.'

Marcus laughed and Lucy noticed that he had taken a far more flattering black suit, which, of course, fitted him perfectly, flattering every muscle, accentuating every single one of his abs.

'We can't all be Batman,' he said flicking his towel off her shoulder and she snorted.

'Batman, really?'

'Don't you think so?' He feigned insult.

More like an Olympic swimmer in one of those full bodysuits before they were banned, she thought but didn't say it aloud. But looking ridiculous was better than being exposed; she

might be tempted to touch him, but this Smurfy
suit would definitely be a turn-off for him.

They boarded the boat with some other guests
and took the short trip out to a smaller island, re-
nowned for its unspoilt coral. As she had done
on the bus trip, she engaged the others in conversation and asked them what had brought them
to the reef. She had to keep making herself remember this wasn't a minibreak with her beau
but a work trip.

After a quick lesson or refresher with the snor-
kel and mask, Ela pointed them in the direction
of the best spots and left them to explore. Lucy
sat on the white sand and put on her flippers. She
stood, but when she tried to walk, she stumbled.

Something, or someone, strong, grabbed her
arm and held her steady for long enough for her
to regain her balance. She looked to the side and
saw Marcus there with a smile that was holding
back a laugh.

'Turn around—you'll find it easier to walk
backwards,' Ela suggested and Lucy obeyed.
Next to her, Marcus had also turned and together
they backed slowly into the clear warm water.

'We look ridiculous,' he teased.

'Speak for yourself, Batman,' she retorted.

'Hey, at least I'm not a Smurf.'

They looked at each other and burst out laugh-
ing.

Once they were waist deep in water, they lifted

their feet and began to paddle. She wondered if Marcus was hiding a fear of the ocean too, but if either of them was, it was Lucy herself. A large grey fish swam within a foot of Lucy and she flung her limbs around in a panic, almost as though her body was trying to throw itself out of the water. Marcus lifted his mask and grabbed her arm. 'It's just a fish, probably more scared of you.'

She felt like a goose. 'I know, I just...' She didn't want to admit that her first thought had been that it was a shark, especially since Ela had already told them that if they did see a shark, it would be harmless and that they shouldn't panic.

'It's just strange being here, in the water with them, that's all.'

'Yeah,' he said and nodded. 'But also kind of amazing. Stay relaxed and calm. I'll be right with you.'

They swam next to one another, paddling and then floating at times over the spectacular reef. They passed fish of all shapes, sizes and colours. Lucy didn't have a hope of identifying a fraction of them, though she knew the stripy black, silver and yellow bannerfish and the striking orange-spotted filefish. The coral stretched on and on, like an exotic garden, coloured in vibrant greens and striking pinks. The lapping sound of the water was calming and soothing. It was amazing how the creatures barely registered Lucy and

Marcus's presence in their world. Lucy felt at one with the ocean.

She could have floated there forever, but eventually Marcus pointed to the beach and they swam back in.

When the water became too shallow to swim, Lucy stood. She tried walking forward with her flippers, instantly remembered the training and turned back to face the azure ocean. She walked backwards towards the beach, with her eyes still on the breathtaking sea.

Suddenly her shoulder made contact with a large, solid mass. She half turned, tripped and lost her balance. Her arms spun but the only thing to hold on to was the thing she had hit. Warm, hard. Definitely male. And not as immovable as it had seemed a second earlier. The solid male mass fell with her and the next thing she knew she was back in the shallow water, facedown. On top of Marcus.

'Oof!' she muttered, winded.

They were a tangle of limbs and flippers. Lucy struggled to get up, but something was snagged. Her mask or his. It didn't even matter; they were stuck. And the more she wiggled, the more their bodies rubbed against one another's. Skin-tight fabric against skin-tight fabric. The more she moved, the more she felt him. Warm, solid. *Very* solid.

'Relax, Lucy. Just let me.' Marcus reached up

between them to unclip whatever it was holding them together. He slid his hand between them, brushing against her chest. His eyes widened for a moment, then he withdrew his hands. But instead of pushing her away as she'd expected, he lifted his hand to her face, brushed an errant lock of hair from her eyes. The world stopped and her body filled with happy hormones. A smile tickled his lips and his gaze fell to hers. That smile gave an awful lot away, and the look in his eyes told her that he had noticed hers as well. Then mortifyingly, she ran her tongue over her own lips. She realised her own body language was also yelling 'lips' and 'kiss' and Marcus lifted his face just enough to brush his smile against hers.

It was a light brush only, but enough to send every one of her cells onto alert, then he drew back.

No. No. Don't stop.

Lucy tilted her face slightly, brushing her lips back over his, causing him to press his mouth firmly, deliberately, resolutely to hers. His tongue swept along hers, sending tingles from her mouth to her toes. Sand everywhere in between. It was too late, all over. She was lying on top on him, their tongues entwined. She let go of the last of her reservations in a loud sigh and felt his arms tighten around her. Why had she been fighting this? It seemed so stupid to have resisted. Marcus, under her, was warm and, oh, so right.

'Okay, you two, take it to the bedroom.'

Ela's voice startled her away from the paradise she was in and back to regular, normal paradise.

Lucy pulled back and they came apart easily. As though they had never been stuck together. She rolled off Marcus and pulled herself up into a sitting position in the sand. She tugged off her flippers and Marcus, now standing and also flipper free, offered her his hand and help to stand. Lucy looked at the offered hand and paused. More skin contact with Marcus probably wasn't a good idea. At least not when she could still taste his sweet mouth in hers, not when her pulse rate was still at maximum and every part of her was tight with desire.

'Let me help you,' he said huskily, and her arm lifted, almost on its own accord.

As soon as she was upright, his fingers released hers and he turned away.

Awkward.

He didn't know where to look. But then again, nor did she.

'Was that okay?'

Okay? It was amazing. It was knee shaking, earth tilting… But he wasn't asking about his kissing skills. Presumably he was well aware of how well he kissed. He was asking whether it was all right that he *had* kissed her.

'It was more than just okay.'

'Lucy, I meant…'

She shook her head. 'I know what you meant and in case you didn't notice, I was a willing participant.'

'There's a "but".'

Of course there was a 'but'. There was the obstacle he knew about—the fact that she worked for him. Then there were the ones he didn't even know about—Lachie, Marcus's decision not to have children…

'Marcus, that was…' Were there even words sufficient describe the feeling of uninhibited desire that has rushed through her as she lay on top of him? Sexy, exciting… She sighed. 'Marcus, it's complicated.'

His wet hair flopped across his high forehead and he pushed it back. His hair was slick and dark and he looked like a movie star from the 1940s. He nodded. 'I know. Look, if you'd like, we can just forget about it.'

Fear gripped her stomach.

'I don't think I could ever forget that' she replied. She wanted to remember that kiss until the day she died. Vividly. In full colour and a zillion pixels.

A smile spread over his face like a sunrise, slowly, but so bright.

She wanted to kiss those magnificent lips again, but didn't know if she'd be able to stop next time. 'I need some time to process it.'

'Of course. That's probably wise.'

Wise. No one had ever called Lucy Spencer wise. Reckless, careless, yes, but never wise.

The others were already back on the boat. Lucy collected her equipment and followed Marcus to join them. Her limbs didn't feel like her own. Her mind and thoughts were floating somewhere above her body.

It was a kiss. Just a kiss. And an accidental kiss at that. A sophisticated, carefree woman of the world would just shrug such a thing off. Move on with her life, as though that sort of thing happened all the time and made no more impact on her life than what she'd eaten for lunch.

Lucy feared she wasn't that sort of woman. And besides, Marcus was not the sort of man you could just kiss and walk away from without a backwards glance.

But like she'd said to him, it was complicated. And he had no idea how complicated it really was.

CHAPTER ELEVEN

BY THE TIME the boat had delivered them back to the island, the sun was low on the horizon.

Ela helped them to the shore and announced, 'There's a tradition of sunset drinks on the patio. Sit back, enjoy a drink and watch the sunset over the ocean. Unless, of course, you wish to stay in your villa.' She looked at him and Lucy when she said that. Or maybe that was his imagination.

It was more than just okay... I was a willing participant.

They were words he liked the sound of. But complicated? Complicated was... Yes, it was complicated. They worked together; he was her boss. But he'd always been able to keep his emotions under control at work. Detached. And if she was a willing participant? And if this was just going to be a fling, while they were here? And if she could also keep her emotions detached too, then maybe it wasn't as complicated as she thought?

The complications might be overcome much more easily than the desire that was overwhelming his veins, that was saturating his senses. Each time he blinked he was overcome with memories of the kiss, of Lucy's soft body writhing on top of his with only that thin, ridiculous fabric between them. Leaving next to no room for his imagination to know what was under it. He shook himself back to reality at the sound of Ela's voice.

'If you wish to eat in your villa, please let us know and we can bring your dinner to you.'

Marcus turned to Lucy. 'What do you think?'

'I think I want to see the sunset from the patio. And I'm happy to eat there too.'

Yes, very wise Lucy. He hadn't been thinking with his head just then. The tropical air must be getting to him. He was her boss. She was his employee. They didn't need to be alone in their villa any more than was necessary.

An hour later, they had both showered and changed. Marcus into fresh shorts and a shirt, and Lucy into a pretty blue dress. His mouth went dry when he saw her—no small feat in this humidity. Her blue dress was designed with a simple classic cut. Sleeveless, with a V-neck, it flared out at the waist to land just below her knees. A simple dress, but on her, it was transformed, magical. The two layers of thin fabric worked together and skimmed over her legs like air. The neckline dipped to just between her breasts, revealing her just-sun-kissed skin. Her usually straight hair fell to her shoulders in gentle waves.

Noticing him watching, self-consciously Lucy touched her hair. 'The salt water has done something to it. It won't stay straight.'

'I think it looks lovely.' It did. He was just being honest, but ever since the kiss they had been in this strange limbo. His original plan, to look and not touch, was not going to work. Now that they *had* kissed he could no longer pretend that whatever it was that lay between them was in his own imagination. Lucy had kissed him back. With gusto. With passion.

A willing participant.

But what did she *think*? She hadn't told him she wanted to forget the whole thing. She hadn't slapped him across the face either. She hadn't resigned or demanded to go home.

She's still getting her head around this too.

For all he knew the kiss might have taken her completely by surprise. She was not privy to all the thoughts he'd been having these last few weeks; she didn't know what was going in his head and how he'd been battling to keep his emotions—and hands—to himself.

She needed time and he would be guided by her.

Living on the eastern coast of a continent, it wasn't often he had the opportunity to see the golden orb of the sun dip below the calm horizon of the ocean, but tonight they did. They marvelled at the reds and oranges and blues that lit the sky until the last of the rays faded and they moved into the restaurant to eat. Over dinner they talked about work. They thrashed over other famous campaigns, covered a lot of the ground they had already, but he didn't care because they were focusing on what they were meant to be thinking about—the pitch. And while they were doing that, they weren't talking about the kiss. The long, slow...kiss, her body pressed up against the full length of his firm frame. Her body, feather light on top of him, but he could sooner have lifted a car off himself than willingly let go of Lucy.

A loved-up Japanese couple sat at the table next to them. In the flickering candlelight he could see all the other guests were also coupled up.

This island was so romantic. What on earth had he been thinking?

He had to focus on work so he didn't focus on Lucy.

Once their gourmet meal and bottle of Tasmanian Pinot were finished, Lucy yawned and immediately covered her mouth, looking embarrassed. 'I'm sorry. I'm having a good time—it's just late.'

'Come on, it was a long day.' He stood and ushered her out. The path up the hill to their villa was lit by lanterns. Someone should really ask them to dial down the romance vibe.

Snorkelling, travelling, not to mention that ride in a helicopter no bigger than a matchbox. And again, Lucy hadn't called him out on his phobia, just quietly, strongly, held his hand. She understood, without being told. Importantly, she didn't make a big deal of it. As they left the restaurant, the memory of her hand in his made him take hers now, without analysing whether it was a good idea or not. They made their way up the lantern-lit path to the villa.

He waited for her to take her hand away, but she didn't. She squeezed his lightly, almost imperceptibly, but his entire body was alert to her movements. He could practically feel each breath she took rippling across his skin.

'I think you were on to something last night. Fiji really is a romantic destination.' She let out a little sigh.

'Maybe we need to do a little more market research?' he suggested and stopped walking, throwing the last of his caution to the balmy evening breeze.

Her pinks lips curled into an alluring grin. Her brown eyes, opened, flashed knowingly for a second.

She had been a willing participant. She hadn't said she didn't want to kiss him, only that it was complicated. And maybe once they shared another kiss they would both realise that maybe, just maybe, things were not as complicated as they thought.

He tugged her hand, pulling her closer and they stood face-to-face. He stroked the soft skin of the back of her hand with his thumb and saw the shiver cross her shoulders. Every other thought left his mind, every other consideration, every other desire. There was only one: Lucy.

He leaned in and his lips found hers. Her mouth opened and welcomed him right away, and a silent cry of *Yes* surged through him. Unlike on the beach, where the kiss had been tentative and public, now they were in semidarkness. The only other people around them were too absorbed in their own romances to pay any attention to Marcus and Lucy.

His heart danced as her hands slid up his chest, over his shoulders and around his neck. He pulled her lean body into his, and when a soft moan escaped her swollen lips, his self-control hung from the barest thread.

'Should we go back to the villa?' he asked, his voice huskier, needier than he would have liked.

'Maybe,' she panted.

Then he remembered. He remembered that while thoughts of sleeping with Lucy had entertained his mind, at a more sensible moment he'd realised that was a big step to take. He'd promised himself that this was not why he'd asked Lucy to come away with him, and to prove that fact, he hadn't brought protection. He drew back slightly.

'You see, the thing is, I don't have any condoms...'

Lucy drew back too, also out of breath. Her chest

heaved and the sight of this put further pressure on his restraint.

'No, no, and it's okay. I mean, it's probably for the best.'

Whether it was for the best would remain to be seen.

He was on the brink of saying, *I could call Reception...* But before he could suggest it, Lucy said, 'We don't know each other very well.'

That was true, and it wasn't. 'I'm not hiding anything from you Lucy. I like you. I like you a lot. But I understand it's complicated—you work for me. I don't want to put you in a position where you feel at all pressured or... I would never hurt you. I want you to know that.'

She looked down and nodded. He wondered if he saw a tear glisten in her soft brown eyes.

The walk back to the villa was quick and in silence. Thoughts jumped around his head, while blood pounded through his veins.

'Lucy, are you okay?' He touched her arm, but she pulled it back.

'I don't really know how to answer that. It's... it's complicated.'

'I know—we work together. Is that it?'

She pressed her lips together and shook her head. What was it she was hiding? What was so damn complicated? They would hardly be the first boss/employee to have a relationship and nor would they be the last.

'Then what?'

She didn't speak for a long time. At least long enough for Marcus to realise that the lines of boss and potential lover were now becoming blurred and that the question he had just asked probably wasn't appropriate for him to be asking.

'Sorry, it's none of my business.'

'Marcus, it's just that…'

He shook his head. 'I understand.'

She pulled a face.

'I do understand that it isn't any of my business. I'm sorry for prying.' He had secrets, things he didn't want anyone knowing. He had reservations too. Maybe not enough. Maybe she was right to keep her cards close.

'Lucy, I'm not looking for a relationship.'

'Nor am I,' she said quickly.

'What I'm trying to say is…'

What was he trying to say? That he just wanted something physical? Because that sounded all wrong and it wasn't true. Not with Lucy. He valued their time together too much; he valued her thoughts, her ideas, her company.

'Look, I like you a lot and…'

Lucy lifted her finger and pressed it to his lips. He fought the urge to kiss it.

'Marcus, listen to me… I like you too. I also don't want a relationship. I think we can be adults, admit there's an attraction here and leave it at that.'

She stepped back and the skin on his arms went cold. He wanted to hold her, pull her close in the same way he needed the sun. In the same way he needed water.

'I think it's best if I call it a night—it was a big day.'

He couldn't argue and he watched her and her blue dress go down the short corridor to her room.

Marcus lay his face in his palms and groaned. Not even the most luxurious villa on the South Pacific was big enough to contain his desire for Lucy. Going to a tropical paradise with a fascinating woman he was struggling to keep his hands off? What had he been thinking?

CHAPTER TWELVE

I THINK WE can be adults, admit there's an attraction here and leave it at that.

Lucy hoped she'd sounded calm and sophisticated, but inside she was a trembling mess. Even now, in the morning, a full twelve hours later, her body was still throbbing from his touch, craving more. Thank goodness their heads had prevailed. If they hadn't stopped when they had, she wasn't sure she would've been able to.

She'd wanted to keep going. To surrender to his touch and his kisses. To let go.

Lucy wasn't a virgin she had a mini-person as evidence of that fact but it had been a long time since she'd done anything that could possibly have created another person. Alex had been her first and only, and that relationship hadn't been what anyone would call a raging success. While she would never regret having Lachie, she had many regrets over Alex. They had both been too young and naive to navigate their relationship after Lachie successfully. Alex had been supportive to begin with, and for a while they had planned a future together, but in the way only seventeen-year-olds who haven't had much experience in the realities of life can.

She had loved Alex. And she knew that he had

honestly once loved her. But her experience with Alex had taught her that sometimes, no matter how much you wanted it to be otherwise, love wasn't always strong enough to withstand what life hurled at it. If she hadn't become pregnant, maybe their love would have been strong enough to last. But very few relationships were strong enough to survive an unplanned teenage pregnancy, and one set of parents who disapproved and openly meddled.

Lucy zipped up her suitcase, picked up her handbag, did a last check of her room before she wheeled the suitcase out to the living room. She was relieved to be getting home and back to Lachie. Glad to be leaving the complication of last night behind. And yet?

After two days and nights, Fiji was starting to feel like her world. And after two days of almost constant contact with Marcus, he was starting to feel like her new normal.

Except he wasn't hers. And this wasn't normal. It was just a bubble. Sydney was real. Lachie was real. The fantasy life of being with Marcus was coming to an end and it was for the best. Just like it was for the best that they had stopped things when they had last night.

Marcus didn't look up from his phone when she entered the room. Which was also a good thing. Her stomach leapt each time she saw even the back of his head; when her eyes met his it practically backflipped.

Lucy looked out the window at the spectacular view. Missing it already.

Marcus sighed. 'This isn't good.'

'What's not?' Had something happened at work?

'A volcanic eruption. In Indonesia.'

Lucy's heart stilled. That was bad, to be sure, but it wasn't affecting them directly. 'That's no good. Have a lot of people died?'

He shook his head. 'None, as far as I know, but the ash is causing all sorts of grief for the aviation industry.'

Lucy's heart paused.

'It isn't safe to fly, apparently, and they might be cancelling some flights,' Marcus said.

'From here?' Lucy hadn't seen any news since she'd been here, too wrapped up in Marcus and their adventures. She had no idea what was happening in the rest of the world.

'From Nadi, yes. It seems so.'

'But when? Not today?' The helicopter they had caught yesterday was meant to fly them directly to Nadi airport, where they would board the flight back to Sydney this afternoon. Surely their flights would be unaffected. The sky out the wide windows now was impossibly clear and blue. Indonesia was so far away.

Marcus clicked on a few more web pages and

scanned his screen. 'It looks like it. Our flight hasn't been cancelled yet, but the airline site is saying that there'll be no more flights leaving today,' he replied.

No. That couldn't be right. 'Please check again. And I'll ring the airline.'

Marcus looked at her properly for the first time. His expression serious. 'Have you had breakfast?'

She shook her head. She didn't feel hungry. Food was the last thing she needed at the moment.

'They've put out a beautiful spread on the balcony. Why don't you get something and I'll make the call?'

Her face must have looked stricken. 'Lucy? Are you all right?'

'I'm worried about the volcano.'

'Lucy, it'll be fine. We're completely safe here.'

It wasn't her immediate safety she was worried about. It was being away from Lachie for even longer than she had been. Not knowing when they'd be back home. Stuck here. *Indefinitely.*

'Have something. A coffee. I'll see what I can find out.'

Lucy obediently went out to the balcony. Her temples felt tight. The smell of strong coffee hit her nostrils. Yes, caffeine. That would make everything better. She poured a cup and took out her phone to see what she could find out. It was one of the biggest stories that morning. 'Volcano. Ash. Sky. Havoc.'

She scrolled in disbelief. She'd heard about this happening in the past. But it was something that happened elsewhere. To other people.

Airports in Australia were already in chaos, but surely they were too far away here?

Marcus stepped out onto the balcony.

'It's all sorted.'

'Our flight's still scheduled?'

'No, our flight from Nadi has been cancelled, but the resort said we can stay here as long as we like.'

No, no, no! He almost looked pleased, but Lucy's heart was thumping and her throat was closing over.

'Cancelled? Are you sure?'

'Yes, I've spoken with the airline. The last flight out of Nadi leaves in one hour. The flights will be grounded after that, no more flights in or out after that. Probably for at least forty-eight hours.'

Lucy stood. 'Then we need to get that earlier flight.'

'It's fine—your boss says it's okay if you're back a few days late.' He gave her one of his winning grins. The same one that had turned her knees to liquid last night. Now it made her heart seize.

'No, you don't understand. We need to get back. I need to get back.'

'Lucy, our flight's been cancelled.'

'But we could get on the earlier one, if you call them.'

She was fighting to get air into her lungs. Why was the air suddenly so heavy? Marcus approached her, put his hand on her shoulder.

'Lucy? What's wrong?'

She pushed him away and stepped back but she still couldn't breathe.

'Lucy, sit. Please. Try to take some slow, deep breaths. You're safe. We're safe. We will work from here. It will all be okay.'

She shook her head. 'I have to get home to my son.'

CHAPTER THIRTEEN

Marcus phoned the airline back immediately and
while he was on hold he emailed Tara to see if
she could get ahold of someone faster. Then he
tried another airline, but the answers were all the
same. Lucy called the helicopter charter company
to see how quickly they could get to Nadi, and by
the sound of her voice she wasn't happy with the
answers she was being given. And all the time
he was on hold, he tried not to think too much
about what Lucy had just told him.

On one hand he was shocked, glad he had the
physical and mental distraction of phone calls and
travel sites to occupy him as he went through the
motions of calling airlines and checking websites.
On the other hand, it wasn't shocking at all. It did,
now he thought about it, make perfect, obvious
sense. It was the missing piece of the Lucy puzzle. The reason she left early, worked late. It was
the reason she was so together. The reason why
as one of the youngest members of his staff, she
seemed like the most mature.

It was, in hindsight, so obvious, he almost felt
like an idiot for not figuring it out sooner.

You didn't figure it out because she lied to you.
Had she?

He pressed Search Flights for the tenth time, on

the tenth airline, and hoped there would be something, anything out of Nadi. Even if they had to go through Brisbane. Or Melbourne. But as he searched he could see flights across the country being cancelled. Even if they could get to Nadi, they'd be stuck there.

She hadn't told him she had a son.

As her boss, he knew he had no right to ask anything. He didn't need to know and he certainly wasn't allowed to treat her any differently. As his employee, she was completely entitled *not* to tell him.

But as his friend? Why didn't she tell him? Why didn't she say something when he first suggested they come to Fiji? Or in the airport lounge when he'd gone on and on about how he never wanted kids?

What did you expect her to say at *that* moment? *Oh, you've just told me you don't like kids and I have one?*

And then they'd kissed and still she'd said nothing, but again…maybe that wasn't the time or the place.

It's complicated.

That's what she'd meant when she'd said it was complicated. Not because he was her boss. He was such a fool.

No one at Oracle had kids. No one he *knew* had kids. At least no one he had much contact with anyway. Mates who married and procreated generally fell off his radar.

She could have told you. You would have understood. He almost laughed at the thought. He hated to admit it to himself, but if Lucy had told him at her first interview that she had a kid, he would not have considered her for the position. The thought made him so uncomfortable he paced the room. He didn't mean to be a jerk, but it would have been a jerk move, not to mention illegal!

He saw himself as Lucy saw him and he didn't like what was reflected back at him.

'Marcus?' The sound of his name brought him back to the room, back to Lucy and the webpage that wouldn't load.

'The charter flight company say their only helicopters are an hour away. They couldn't get here and get us to Nadi in time, even if they wanted to.'

'I can't get us on any flight out of Nadi anyway, so it doesn't matter.'

Lucy swallowed and he was almost sure she was about to cry. He stood and went to her but she stepped back.

'It's not your fault,' she said.

Marcus clenched his fists. It felt like his fault.

If he hadn't been such a workaholic running a family-unfriendly office, she would have told him. If he hadn't been so judgemental about other people with children, she might have felt comfortable telling him. If he hadn't been such a blind jerk…

'Is it okay if I call him?'

'Of course, take as long as you want. I'll just go for a walk.' He had to get out of this villa. For one of the most luxurious on the Coral Coast, it suddenly felt far too small.

Lucy found him sitting at a table in the cafe at the main pavilion, with a view over the lagoon. The view was as beautiful as the one from their villa. A few other guests lingered over a late breakfast. Marcus sat hunched over his laptop. She took a deep breath and approached him.

'Do you mind if I join you?'

He shook his head and attempted a smile, but he wasn't looking forward to this conversation any more than she was.

They ordered two coffees and once the waiter left, Lucy began, 'I'm so sorry I didn't tell you.'

'You didn't have to—it's none of my business.'

Lucy paused. That was a bit blunt. She thought he might be a bit more affected. Not angry, she didn't want him to be angry. But she thought he might have cared, somehow.

'I'm sorry I didn't tell you as your friend.' Were they friends? They were colleagues, friends, almost lovers. They had many potential relationships. Or none at all. 'I should have told you. I was lying.'

'No, you just didn't tell me the truth. And you didn't have to.'

What was he saying? He was being too reasonable. Yes, as his employee she didn't have to tell him anything about her personal life, but she thought they had passed the traditional boss/subordinate barrier a few days ago. And certainly after yesterday.

'I wasn't up-front with you. And I want to explain why. Even if you say it's none of your business, I would like you to know.'

His expression softened, his features turning from stone to their usual engaged mode.

'I would be very grateful if you heard me out,' she said.

He nodded and closed his laptop.

Under the table, Lucy twisted her hands together. 'At first I was worried that you wouldn't hire me.'

Marcus placed his face in his hands.

'I desperately wanted the job. I couldn't afford to take any chances'

'Of course. I understand.'

'You're not angry?'

'Only at myself. I'm so sorry, Lucy.'

'What for?'

He took his hands away from his face. 'I know it would've been wrong, but I can't say, hand on heart, that it wouldn't have made a difference if you'd told me at the interview.'

'Oh.' Lucy reeled. 'Does that mean…you don't want me at Oracle anymore?'

Marcus stood and reached over to her, grabbing her arm. Almost as if he was trying to pull her back. 'No, no, no. That's not it at all. No, Lucy, please don't go anywhere. I only meant that if I'd known from the beginning I may have been reluctant to hire you and that would have been wrong. So wrong.'

'What are you saying?'

'Lucy, I've never even worked with anyone who has kids. I don't think that was intentional, but it hasn't happened. But you're the most dedicated, hardworking employee I've ever had.'

She scoffed.

'It's true. You're focused, diligent. And you are also immensely talented. I would have been a fool not to hire you.'

It was a lot to take in. Marcus wasn't angry at her—but only at himself. This wasn't a scenario she'd imagined. The distress on his face was apparent. 'Oh, I've really messed this up.'

'I think we both have,' she said. 'I'm sorry I didn't tell you the truth.'

He held her gaze and shook his head sadly. 'I'm sorry you felt like you couldn't.'

'What now?'

'Now we should talk. Whatever you want to

tell me, I'll hear it. And then maybe I can learn what I can do better. Teach me.'

Lucy exhaled, looked at the view for a long moment. Was she really going to tell him everything? She had to, and not just to explain her past actions, but because she needed Marcus to know everything. She needed him to know for the future. If they were going to have one.

'I wanted to pretend. I know that sounds awful, but I wanted to fit in at Oracle. I wanted to be treated like everyone else. I love Lachie with all my heart, but I've missed out on so many things.'

'What do you mean?'

Lucy stared her coffee, even though it didn't need stirring. This was it. Maybe even worse than telling Marcus about Lachie in the first place.

'You see...' This was the thing she really didn't want to tell him. This was the point where Marcus was going to judge her. It would change everything he thought or felt about her. Whatever might have been smouldering between them would be snuffed out completely.

'You see, Lachie is five years old.'

She let her gaze rest on his shoulder, not directly enough to see the full reaction, fearing it would hurt too much. But she still needed to see the moment of realisation, the moment it hit him. The moment everything changed between them forever.

Marcus's eyes flickered and she saw the moment dawning. Before he could ask, she said.

'I was seventeen when I got pregnant.'

Marcus's face shuttered. He was a good actor. A passer-by would not have noticed the way his lips pressed together a little more than usual. Or the way his eyelids twitched. He swallowed three times in thirty seconds. She sat in silence and counted.

'That must have been hard,' he said eventually.

'It wasn't easy. My parents were great. They still are.' She didn't want to mention Alex and Marcus didn't ask.

He just nodded and said, 'I'm sorry you didn't feel you could tell us. Me.'

Marcus reached across the table and picked up her hands. He cradled them in hers.

This was strange. Definitely not the reaction she'd been expecting. He was sad, but he wasn't angry. Certainly not at her. She watched their two pairs of hands wrapped in one another. It was easier than looking at his face.

'I just wanted to pretend for a bit. Pretend to be as carefree as everyone else in the office. I didn't expect it to go on for so long. You probably think it's selfish, lying about my son. I just wanted not to be the teenage mother for once. Not have to hear the judgement, the insults.'

'Insults?'

She laughed. 'Are you kidding? The sideways

glances. The narrowed eyes. The questions. *Are you his sister? His nanny? His mother? But how old are you? That was a pretty irresponsible thing to do.*'

Marcus met her gaze and held it. 'I'm sorry you had to go through that.'

He kept saying that. Almost like he was somehow to blame. For something. Maybe he was just apologising for what he was going to do. For the fact that this surely meant the end of whatever it was between them. The end of the kissing. The end of the tension.

'Marcus, you have nothing to be sorry about. And I'm sorry I didn't tell you last night and I completely understand that this changes things.'

'Yeah, well.' Marcus let go of her hands and placed his own in his lap.

Her heart crashed to the ground. She'd known on one level—the logical, sensible plane—that Marcus would not be attracted to her now he knew about Lachie, but the rejection still stung. And it stung more than she'd expected.

She stood and he looked up in question.

'What are you going to do now?' he asked.

'I don't know. Go back to my room.'

His brow furrowed. 'Do you have to make arrangements? Is your son... Lachie—he's safe and cared for?'

'He's fine. He's with my parents. He's having a great time.'

Marcus stood too. 'Then maybe we should see what else we can try? Maybe take a glass-bottom dinghy to explore the lagoon?'

'Really?'

'Of course, but if you don't want to, I understand.'

She nodded. 'I'd like to. And I want to do something, get out of here. Unless you need to work?'

Maybe Marcus wasn't angry at all, just surprised, like he said. This might be the end of the attraction between them, but it didn't mean they couldn't be friends.

'I think we should make the most of our time here, don't you?' he said.

The kitchen packed them a picnic hamper for lunch and they borrowed one of the resort's glass-bottomed boats. They spent the rest of the morning navigating the turquoise lagoon in a glass-bottomed dinghy, admiring the brightly coloured coral and the cheeky schools of tropical fish.

As they passed over a shoal of coral fish, Lucy gasped.

'What is it?' he asked.

'Shhh,' she said and gripped his arm.

'What?' His skin prickled. He knew he should be looking at the wonders below them but at that moment he only wanted to enjoy the sensation of Lucy's small hand wrapped around his bare arm.

She nodded to starboard. Beneath the boat passed an enormous green turtle. With its unmistakable black-spotted face and limbs, it glided past their boat. Close enough to touch. They sat perfectly still and in silence as they watched the magnificent ancient creature coast under the boat. Lucy kept her hand on his arm the entire time.

Marcus pointed to the other side of the boat. There were half a dozen more, of all ages and sizes, swimming towards them. They sat, in wonder, until the group had passed.

'That was magical,' she said. Marcus nodded and simply smiled at her. His heart was full of Lucy and the time they were sharing. 'I wish Lachie had seen that,' she said, then her cheeks flushed pink and she looked away from him as though she regretted mentioning her son. It wasn't right he'd made her feel like she couldn't even mention her son in his presence, but he had no idea how to make her more comfortable. He had no idea how to even talk about children, let alone how to act around them.

They landed the dinghy at one of the beaches. A private beach, a gourmet picnic. A beautiful woman. Marcus lay back in the sand and stared up at the sky. It was so clear and blue it was strange to think that planes across the Southern Hemisphere had been grounded due to ash.

But they had been. And he'd finally learnt Lucy's secret.

A kid. A son she'd been taking care of for the last five years. It explained so much about Lucy and why she was the way she was.

Mature, efficient, gorgeous…

No. That's what you thought before you knew she had a kid.

Did knowing about her son change anything? She was still attractive, sweet, sexy. He still wanted her, he realised with a jolt.

Nothing *had* actually changed. There was never any possibility of a long-term thing between them, so knowing she was a mother didn't change that now.

Something had changed, though. His respect for Lucy had increased tenfold. She'd finished school and university all the while raising her son. He felt nothing but admiration for her.

That uncomfortable feeling still gnawed at him. Guilt. He was a workaholic and he had assembled an office full of them. He hadn't made Oracle the kind of place where his employees felt they could tell him something like that. He hadn't created an open and diverse company. And he didn't like that realisation about himself one little bit.

'Are we going to eat or just lie here?' Lucy asked, lying next to him. 'Because either way is fine with me. I could happily nod off.'

'We should probably eat,' he replied, but he

didn't move. It was so relaxing in the sun. It felt
like they'd been given this day.

He sensed Lucy rummaging through the basket. 'Oh, my!' she exclaimed.

'What?'

'Champagne.' She held up a bottle. 'Can you
believe it?'

He could. OZ had organised a trip so luxurious
it would inspire them to create one of the greatest
ad campaigns ever made. The Angel Isle Resort
had got the memo. Lucy pulled out fresh prawns,
tropical fruit, fresh salads and bread and laid it
on the picnic blanket.

'This feels so decadent. It feels like we're skip-
ping school or something.'

'There's nothing wrong with that once in a
while,' Marcus said.

Lucy smiled sadly. 'It's hard for me to think
of it that way.'

'What do you mean?'

'I mean, I wish I hadn't had to miss so much
school. I didn't get the luxury of skiving off for
leisure purposes. I didn't even get to take days
off when I was sick. All the time I've ever had off
has been to have and then to look after Lachie.'

'Hardly irresponsible, then. Whatever people
might have said.'

She twirled her foot in the sand and nodded.

'Yep. Irresponsible, unreliable. Those are the
nicer things.' She laughed. 'They've said far worse.'

He didn't want to ask what they'd said; sadly he thought he knew. He hated to think how it must have been for her, yet part of him wanted to know more. It was selfish really, since he had no right to. And he wasn't even sure why he wanted to know more. But he did.

'And I don't suppose they ever said that sort of thing to Lachie's father?'

She shook her head.

'Is he still in Lachie's life?'

'When it suits him to be.'

Marcus frowned. 'He doesn't live in Sydney?'

'Yes, he does. Two suburbs away. He's meant to have him every second weekend.'

'But?'

'You really want to know?' Lucy looked up at him and the look in her big eyes could have broken a thousand hearts.

'Only if you want to tell me. And not as your boss. Or anything else. As your friend.'

CHAPTER FOURTEEN

'WE WERE IN high school. His name was—is—Alex. We'd known each other for years, been in the same classes, had some of the same friends. I'd never thought of him like that, you know, romantically, until the dance at the end of year ten.'

Lucy had liked Alex as a friend and had agreed happily to dance. But something shifted when he held her. It had felt good being held by him. When her mind opened itself to the possibility that they might be more than friends, she didn't dismiss it. And Alex liked her. That in itself was slightly intoxicating. No one had ever held her like that, looked at her like that. The dance led to another, a party afterwards and, after edging closer and closer to one another, in the early hours of the morning, their first kiss.

That heady summer they had been inseparable.

'Anyway, we started seeing each other. It was all very innocent at first. Until it wasn't. Before you ask, we did use a condom. It broke. And, yes, I should have got the morning-after pill but I was seventeen—I wasn't sure how to go about it. I didn't want to tell my mum that not only had we had sex but that the condom had broken. It was only a few days after my period and everything I read seemed to say it would be okay.'

'It wasn't?'

'Well, I got pregnant.'

Lucy looked out over the lagoon, an incongruous view, two thousand miles away from the story she was telling.

'What happened next?' Marcus asked.

'I told Mum first. Even before Alex. I wasn't sure about anything. Mum was great—*is* great. Dad too. Mum said right up she would support me whatever I decided. To continue with the pregnancy. To keep him. To not keep him. To tell Alex, or not.'

'You thought about not telling Alex?'

'I thought about not telling *anyone*. Not even my mother. Just going to the doctor and having a termination. If I didn't tell anyone, I figured it would almost be like it hadn't happened. But…' Lucy shook her head. While on one hand she had wanted it never to have happened, she was also deeply protective of the life inside her. 'I told Mum. Going to the doctor was too scary. The thought of having a baby was scary too, but somehow further into the future. More abstract. Once Mum assured me she'd support me a hundred percent no matter what, I decided to tell Alex. I thought that was only fair and that we'd figure it out together. Like Mum, he said he'd support me whatever I chose. And then we told my Dad. They were all trying to be helpful, by telling me that they'd support me no matter what

I decided. But it meant I had to make the decision. And by the time we all told Alex's parents, well, it was like… I don't know, I guess I'd decided to keep him.'

'And Alex's parents?'

'His mum was okay. His dad, not so much. He didn't tell me to have a termination—not in as many words—but he wasn't happy. And he blamed me. Still does. Still thinks I ruined Alex's life and never misses an opportunity to tell me.'

Marcus frowned deeply and squeezed the champagne cork tightly between his fingers. 'What does Alex do?'

'He's still in Sydney. He's a lawyer now.'

'Really?'

'Yes. His life was not disrupted as his father suggests. If anything…'

'What?'

'If anything, he threw himself into study to avoid other things.' In the beginning, that had been the plan. It made sense for Alex to study, to get good marks in his final year. It didn't make sense for them both to flunk out. If Alex was going to have any hope of supporting them, he needed to finish school and get a good degree. Alex had studied hard, at school and then at university. But it meant he spent less time with Lucy and Lachie and they drifted slowly, easily apart. Despite sharing a son, their lives went in separate directions.

'Oh.'

'I had Lachie in the middle of my final year. Just before my eighteenth birthday. I was hoping so much he would come after my birthday. It's silly, but somehow having a kid at eighteen doesn't sound quite as bad as seventeen.' Lucy didn't dare look at Marcus's face. She'd never confessed that to anyone. She knew, even now that it didn't make a lick of difference. 'We had a plan worked out so that I would still attempt to study. Mum and Dad and Alex and his mum, we were all going to take Lachie one day a week each so I could study. I'd still have him nights and weekends. That was how it was meant to work anyway.'

'But no?'

'Babies don't work to plan. I might have had my days free, but I was exhausted, being up so many nights. Lachie was a pretty good baby, but still. The school was great, but it was clear I was behind. I thought it would be best if I deferred, give Alex more time to study.' Lucy sighed. Summoning all her courage, she turned her head and met Marcus's gaze. He was watching her seriously, intently. His eyes were dark, but Lucy knew his anger wasn't for her. There was so much she could tell him, so much she suddenly wanted to tell him. How angry she'd been at Alex, how disappointed. But how Lachie was suddenly her whole world. She didn't want to be apart from him, physically couldn't bear not to be with him. But not now. Now she focused on the main things.

'We broke up properly once he was at university. It happened slowly—we pretended for a long time, to ourselves, to each other. He's still involved in Lachie's life. He has Lachie every other weekend, mostly, but…he has busy job, a girlfriend.'

'I see.'

Lucy didn't want to sound bitter and she wasn't. At least not about Alex. She had fallen out of love with him a long time ago. While she didn't want him back, the hurt hadn't faded. She tried to keep a check on her resentment. When Alex was excelling at his career, she reminded herself that the extra money was good for Lachie. When Alex had met his girlfriend and entered into a stable relationship with a woman who accepted Lachie and his place in Alex's life, Lucy reminded herself yet again that this could only be good for Lachie.

'So…' Lucy spread her arms. 'Judge away.' It would be better if he just came out and said it. *Reckless, stupid, selfish…*

Marcus didn't say anything for a long time. He kept twirling the cork between his fingers. She wasn't sure if he was avoiding saying something or if he just didn't know what to say.

Finally he put the cork down and said, 'You know, the only reason I didn't have sex when I was seventeen was lack of opportunity, not lack of desire.'

She laughed. 'Really? *That's* your response to everything I just told you?'

'Really, I was moody, pimply. Very awkward.'

'Somehow I find that hard to believe.'

He gazed at her, serious. The thought of them both as sexual beings hung heavy and obvious between them. An oversized elephant making her presence known and felt in her own core.

'What I'm trying to say, badly, is that I can't even imagine what it must have been like. I'm in awe of you.'

Lucy stared at him. 'Don't be ridiculous.'

'I'm not. You did finish school, and you graduated from university.'

'I had a lot of help.'

'I had a lot of help and school and university were *still* hard and I wasn't raising a kid. You sell yourself too short, Lucy. Didn't anyone ever tell you that?'

She shook her head. 'It was my fault, my mistake.'

'Yes and no. You're hardly the first person in the world to have an unplanned pregnancy.'

'I was irresponsible.'

Marcus's face cracked into a funny look, part grin, part grimace.

'Deciding to keep and care for your son isn't irresponsible.'

'But getting pregnant so young was.'

Marcus sat straighter. 'Who tells you that?'

She shrugged. 'The world. Strangers, mothers at school, teachers… Alex's father.'

'For what it's worth, Lucy Spencer, I think you are remarkable.'

She felt lighter, bigger, her chest suddenly full of air. But did he mean that? No one else had ever expressed such pride in her, except for her parents, who had always done so unconditionally. Maybe it was the thought of her parents and their love, or her relief or Marcus's words but tears began to wet behind her eyelids. She turned and brushed them away.

'I had a lot of help.'

'Not from Alex, by the sounds of things.'

'He's busy…'

'He's still a father. He shouldn't shirk his responsibilities.'

They sat on that comment and let the sun kiss their faces. She never would have expected Marcus to say such a thing. Marcus, who never wanted children. Who had told her outright that they were not part of his life plan.

'Is that why you don't want kids?'

Marcus pulled a face. 'What?'

'The responsibility.'

Marcus's eyes darkened. She had stepped too far. Possibly onto a metaphorical crocodile. 'Actually, sorry, no, forget I asked,' she said. 'It was a deeply personal question.' Lucy started clearing away their picnic, wrapping the leftovers, putting lids on containers, tying up the rubbish.

As she put a bag of rubbish into the basket, Marcus stilled her hand with his.

'It isn't that.'

Lucy shook her head. 'That was unbearably rude of me. I'm sorry.'

'Lucy, it's fine. It isn't the responsibility I'm worried about. It's the pain.'

Marcus paused. The pain. He'd never quite articulated his fears like that before, but, to his surprise, it summed it up. The pain, or rather, the *potential* for pain.

'What do you mean?' Lucy moved back from the picnic basket and placed her hands on her bare knees, ready to listen. But Lucy had a child; she didn't want to hear his story of love and loss.

Lucy's a mother. She knows things, has felt things you can only imagine. She's no stranger to pain.

'Actually, I'm not sure I should tell you.'

'It's okay, you don't have to. It's your business. We all have our secrets.' Her smile was forced, but her words were genuine.

Lucy had kept secrets. But not any longer. She had shared her biggest with him. He started his story, without knowing how he would finish it.

'I had a brother, my older brother. His name

was Joel.' Marcus was aware his voice was unsteady, but the only way to get through this was to talk quickly. Get it over with. Like he was ripping off a Band-Aid.

'He was sixteen. I was fourteen. Joel was a daredevil. The kind of kid who would jump first and look later. Joel, Dad and I went out for a bike ride one Sunday morning, like we would often do. To give Mum a sleep-in. Anyway, we were nearly home and riding down a hill near our place, a hill the three of us had ridden down many times before. Joel took the tight, blind corner at the bottom of the hill at speed and...there was an oncoming truck. It didn't see him coming in time. The only good thing we tell ourselves is that it would've all happened so fast, Joel wouldn't have even known. That might be comfort for some, but not my father. He saw his eldest son get cleaned up by a truck just meters in front of him and there was nothing he could do. Joel was already dead by the time Dad got to him.'

'Oh, Marcus that's so awful. I'm so, so sorry.' Lucy wrapped her arms around herself tight, even though the air was balmy and the sun was warm. Marcus had no doubt that, even though Lucy was giving him her full attention, part of her thoughts were with Lachie. Part of her was praying that her son was safe.

'It was awful. I was... The whole time is a

blur for me. But as awful as it was for me, it was worse for my parents.'

Lucy nodded slowly. 'How are they now?'

'Mum's fine. Good, almost. It sounds traitorous to say, but she's good. She was a teacher, but after, she retrained. She's a counsellor now.'

'And your dad?'

'He died. Six years after Joel. He didn't cope.' Martin Hawke had found comfort in drink, but in the way of things, the drink had not saved him. It had consumed him and destroyed him. 'Liver failure, brought on by excessive alcohol.'

Lucy sighed. Then she reached over and placed her hand on his arm. 'I'm so sorry.'

That was all there was to say. His family had halved in size. It was just him and his mother now, which meant he'd already lost most of the people that were dear to him.

Lucy opened her mouth to say something else, but thought better of it and pressed her lips tightly together. She simply squeezed his arm.

They packed up the picnic, climbed back into the boat and set off again. They had a glorious afternoon. The best of the trip. They explored bays and coves and circumnavigated the island. She had never felt closer to Marcus. She sensed that she understood him now, better than ever. He'd shared something deeply personal with her, and she felt warmer knowing that he trusted her. But that was counterbalanced with the knowledge of the sadness he carried around like a weight. Lucy didn't have siblings, so she couldn't quite grasp what it would be like to lose one. But she was a parent, so could easily imagine the grief his parents would have felt—the grief his mother must still feel. Lucy could feel it in her own bones.

It also explained so much about Marcus. The light and the dark, why he wanted the things he did, why he was so driven. So serious.

But it also explained why Marcus never wanted a family. His revelation made her feel as though she'd lost something; any nascent dreams she might have been having of a possible shared future vanished. Marcus was not the man for her; as much as she was attracted to him, as wonderful as he was, no matter how *good* they were together, they could never share a future. But as sad as that was, the knowledge also somehow set her free. Marcus Hawke could never be hers. *Would* never be hers.

She'd never have to tackle the messy juggle of an office romance, never have to decide between her job and Marcus. They would be friends. That was all it was ever meant to be. Their mutual attraction was a fact, but it didn't have to be awkward. It didn't have to be weird.

It just *was*. Now they'd both come clean, laid their respective cards on the table so to speak, they would move on with their lives.

And the attraction? He might make her blood sizzle and her body clench and a whole lot more besides, but that was that.

It was lucky she'd learnt all this now, because if she let herself believe they might stand a chance, she might get her hopes up. She might start to fall...

This way was much safer.

The sun was setting by the time they got back to the resort. Her skin was tight with the sun and salt, her mouth aching from smiling, her muscles relaxed from laughter.

'Would you like sunset drinks up on the patio, or to stay in?' Marcus asked as he tied up the dinghy.

'I'm exhausted,' she replied, and she was. After the stress of the morning they had enjoyed a long day in the sun. Not to mention the champagne on the beach. And several long, personal conversations.

'Then we'll stay in,' he replied.

Which was what she wanted, wasn't it? A relaxing and early night in?

Back at their villa, she showered and changed into shorts and a T-shirt. She called Lachie, who was still having a great time and largely oblivious to her absence. Which might have had something to do with the extra large LEGO set Lucy had asked

her mother to buy to keep him distracted and assuage Lucy's guilt at being away from him for so
long. He would back at school the next day, but
Lucy still had no idea when she would be able to
fly again and when she would be home.

When she came out of her room a three-course
dinner and another bottle of champagne had been
delivered. Marcus had set it all up on the villa's
private deck and they had their own view of the
lagoon under the starlight.

If you had to be stuck anywhere in the world,
she decided, this was probably the place to be.
Marcus had also showered and changed. His dark
hair was still damp and he was wearing a T-shirt
and shorts, just like her. Unlike her, the outfit
didn't look casual on him, but effortlessly sexy.

'Drink?' he offered.

'Yes, please. You know, a girl could get used
to this,' she said as she took the glass and tried
not to think about how Marcus could run a side
hustle as a T-shirt model.

After they had eaten as much as they could,
Lucy stood and began to clear the plates. Marcus reached for her hand. 'Leave it—they'll send
someone.'

'But...' Lucy began. She cleaned and cleared
and wiped and washed by instinct. Because if she
didn't, they would think she was irresponsible,
lazy. Someone who neglected their commitments.

'But nothing,' he insisted.

'I feel guilty,' she admitted and reached for her glass.

He laughed gently and placed his hand over hers. 'This is one of the most exclusive resorts in the country—they'll clear up after us.'

She took a breath so deep it filled her entire torso.

'Would it help if your boss directed you leave it?' Marcus picked up her hand and squeezed it.

She wanted to sigh. No, that wouldn't help. It would only remind her that the man sitting less than a foot away from her, holding her hand in his and surrounding her in his cloud of salt and aftershave and mango and manliness was her boss, decidedly off limits, and not some miraculous stranger with no other connection to her than the intense physical attraction they felt for one another.

He didn't let her go. Even after she nodded her acquiescence. And she didn't take her hand away either. She loved the way her hand felt, held by his. His grip was firm, yet unquestionably careful. It had been so long since she'd been cherished, since someone had put her first. Long-forgotten and suppressed sensations bubbled to the surface. She'd been missing out on these feelings for so long.

If only they could forget everything that lay between them, their roles, Lachie. The rest of the world. Could they, for one night only, just exist on this island and forget the rest of the world? After all, he didn't want anything serious and she couldn't get into anything serious, so didn't that, if you really thought about it, make things perfect?

She leaned closer to him and, miraculously, he let go of her hand, only to slide his arms around her waist and pull her onto his waiting lap. She balanced herself by sliding her arm around him and pulling in close. He was strong and his warmth enveloped her.

Their faces were now level and mere inches apart. Marcus slid his fingers across her chin and his palm came to rest gently cupping her chin. Lucy's entire world shrank to just him and her and their embrace. Marcus ran his thumb across her lips and a thrill skipped down her spine.

'I'm not expecting anything from you,' she said. She needed him to know.

He narrowed his eyes in question.

'I know a family isn't on your agenda.'

Marcus pressed his lips together like he was trying not to say exactly what was on his mind.

Lucy had no such reservations. She realised she needed him to know exactly what she was thinking. *She needed him.* 'With everything going on, I could only do casual.'

'You could only do casual?'

She nodded and kept explaining. 'I'm just not looking for someone, I don't want to bring someone into Lachie's life, not with his father being so unpredictable.'

Marcus's grin made her stomach flip, but it was maddening; she couldn't tell what he was thinking.

'There's nothing wrong with casual, no strings attached. If anything it's the most responsible way for me to be right now. That way, no one gets hurt, not me, not Lachie.'

'Honestly, Lucy. If you want to know what the casual type is—look at me. I'm the poster boy.'

She smiled. He understood what she was saying.

The smile he returned was broad, unquestionably cheeky. 'When you look up *casual* in the dictionary, there's a photo of yours truly. And that movie? *Friends with Benefits*? I inspired that.'

Lucy ran her hand up his arm and squeezed his shoulder. 'Um, didn't that couple get together in the end?'

'I didn't say they followed my example. That couple couldn't do it right—not everyone has my skills.'

He was offering her no-strings-attached sex. Wasn't that exactly what she wanted? To be in Marcus's arms, and his bed, but with none of the messy emotional fallout?

As he lowered his lips to hers, she felt her confidence waiver. She might want a causal relationship, but that didn't mean she had any experience of one. Could she do it? Could she handle working with him after they crossed that line?

'To be honest, I haven't exactly...not since Alex.'

Marcus leaned back and his embrace loosened, thought he still held her securely in his lap. 'Wait, can we rewind a little? Are you saying you haven't...since you two split?'

She blushed. 'I've been busy,' she ground out. 'But that doesn't change anything.'

Being with him was so easy. After their long talk today she felt so comfortable with him, so yes, she could handle this. She wasn't ready to bring someone else into Lachie's life—least of all someone who didn't like children. But she needed this for her. She was a mother, but still a person. She wanted this. She wanted *Marcus*.

She traced her finger from his ear, down his neck and just under his T-shirt. She loved the way his lids lowered as she did. She exhaled, closed her eyes and bridged the last inch left between them.

He didn't need much persuasion; her lips gently opened and his met hers with a moan. His hands slid up her back and tangled into her hair, and every pore in her body opened, wanting to be the one that was blessed with Marcus's caress, or better yet, his mouth. Lucy's muscles became weaker, molten, and her knees began to sway.

Her thoughts leapt forward a few minutes. No,

a few moments. Another caress, another lick and she would be lost. Incapable of judgement. Devoid of common sense.

'Marcus…'

'Um…' he murmured, or was it 'yum'?

'We have to stop now. If we don't, I won't be able to.'

Marcus lifted his lips just far enough from hers to ask, 'Do we have to?'

'We don't have protection.'

He drew his index finger down her cheek and held her gaze. 'What if we did?'

'But we don't and Marcus, I've done the accidental pregnancy thing once. It isn't something I intend to do again.'

He pulled back far enough to study her face with his piercing blue eyes.

'Lucy, we don't have to do anything. But I do have protection.'

'How?'

'Concierge.'

Her mouth fell open.

'It doesn't mean anything—we don't have to do anything.'

Was he saying he didn't want to? That he'd changed his mind? No. This would probably be their only chance. Lucy had missed out on so much over the past five years. She was not going to miss her one chance with Marcus Hawke.

'I haven't changed my mind.' She said it so he'd be sure to understand.

Torn between this moment and what she knew was to come, she slid her fingers into his hair and pulled his mouth back to hers. Their lips moved slowly, as though tasting a new food. A dish at a five-star restaurant. Savouring, searching, identifying each new flavour and texture.

Like a five-course degustation, it was to be savoured, lingered over, not rushed.

Full of fascination and novelty.

They took their time, knowing that they had all night. They had until the planes started flying if necessary. They were stuck here for the foreseeable future. She took the time to linger, smell him, breathe him in. She had time to watch the corners of his lips curl, the lids on his eyes lower. She had time to trace his muscles from his neck to his waist and revel in the way he trembled when she did.

He had time to slide his fingers languidly up her back, from her waist, as though checking each vertebra as he went. His lips lingered above hers for an age, waiting in that moment between one life and the next.

Up close she noticed his eyes were a kaleidoscope of blues. As his gaze flickered over her face, the flecks moved in a hypnotising dance.

It wasn't like she remembered it had been with Alex. Of course she was older, but Marcus knew what he was doing. He knew where to place his hands, just the right amount of pressure, the places that made her muscles contract, shake and melt again.

He knew when to push and when to pull and when to place a kiss just between her breasts. He knew just when they should come together and how to move in just the right way. He knew when to be gentle and when not. And he knew exactly when she would finally come undone. Because he did too.

CHAPTER FIFTEEN

MARCUS WOKE TO a distant buzzing. It was his phone, but it was far away. It took him a moment to orient himself. The sun was high enough in the sky to be filling the room with bright light. Next to him a lusciously naked Lucy lay tangled in the sheets. Her room, her bed. Her arms. He'd left his phone in the other room when, last night, she had led him to her bed and to a night better than anything he'd let himself imagine. Which was just as well. Because if he'd known a month ago what it would be like to be with Lucy, he would not have managed to keep his thoughts straight. As it was now, he wasn't sure how he'd manage.

But at least they'd been honest and open with one another, first about their pasts. He'd told her all about Joel, and Lucy and told him about her son. And they'd been honest about what they wanted from one another—casual, no strings. Neither of them was in a position to offer anything more.

It was a strange feeling. On one hand, he had never felt so content. Being with Lucy was so easy; she was so good to be with. On the other hand, his body didn't seem to fit in his skin anymore. He felt fulfilled one moment, yet consumed by need the next.

He needed her lips, he was addicted to their taste and he wanted to breathe her in with every breath he took. He was obsessed. It was a need, a hunger like a starving man, and like a starving man he was just as desperate, irrational… What was wrong with him? The stress of the pitch—that was all. He'd never pitched for something so big. This was the one.

It must be the stress, the pressure that was making him think like this. Feel like this.

Marcus didn't usually let feelings overtake him.

Thoughts, actions, hard work—that's what got you results.

Doing basic things like answering your damn phone.

One night with Lucy and he was already forgetting to answer his phone?

Marcus extracted himself with regret from Lucy's arms and went to locate his still-ringing phone.

Five minutes later, he was still sitting on his bed, wrapped in a robe and holding his phone. Lucy, also wearing one of the resort's robes, peeked in his open door. Her hair delightfully mussed up from the bed and his fingers, which had spent half the night caressing her.

She was perfection, he thought, with regret.

'What is it?' she asked.

He took a deep breath. 'Good news.' At least

she would think it was. 'The ash has cleared from here at least. We have a flight from Nadi this afternoon.'

He didn't let himself watch the look of relief as it crossed her face. 'Great, that's great,' she replied. 'When do we leave?'

She was happy to leave, so he was too. That's just how things had to be.

They packed silently and gathered their things.

It was good they were going home, wasn't it? Certainly Lucy had thought so. She was desperate to get home to Lachie. He purposefully distracted himself on the helicopter ride with a report Liam and Daphne had sent through overnight. He didn't let himself think about the plunge below.

Neither of them spoke much until they were waiting in the lounge at Nadi, their flight due to leave in fifteen minutes.

Lucy put her coffee mug down, cocked her head and asked, 'Is everything okay?'

Was it? After the night they'd shared, were they about to return to business as if it had never happened? They'd framed it as a night of no-strings fun and yet…suddenly, somehow, this wasn't the man he wanted to be. Apart from anything else, he wanted to see Lucy again. Their different lives meant this thing between them did have an end date, but he didn't want it to be so soon. Not yet.

Still, he was the boss. The employer. And he'd already proven that he was a less than perfect employer by creating a workplace where parents didn't feel welcome.

'Can we talk?' he asked her. Those three words carrying the weight of millions of bad conversations. He quickly added, 'I want to make sure you're okay.'

'I'm fine,' she said but the way her voice grew higher at the end of 'fine' betrayed her.

'I've had a good time. I've had a great time, I'm sorry you had to stay longer than planned, but selfishly, I've had an amazing trip.'

A smile tugged reluctantly at her lips. 'Me too.'

'I don't regret a thing. But I also know our lives are on different trajectories. I'm not going to ask you for anything more.'

She breathed in deeply and nodded. 'I know that. And I'm not looking for anything either.' She picked up his hand and turned it over in her small soft, palms. Deceptively soft. Deceptively small. She was one of the strongest people he'd ever known. To raise a child, practically on her own, as a teenager. Carrying the weight of all that work, and all that worry, alone. He'd known adults not capable of that sort of strength.

'I know you don't want a family,' she said.

Was that true? He didn't want the pressure and responsibility of children. The potential for heartbreak. But was that the same as not *wanting* a family? His heart constricted.

You can't have one without the other.

'I just don't think I'm cut out for it.'

'I'm not sure anyone ever does.'

She stared at him, her demeanour calm, her eyes and her attention focused only on him.

He couldn't back out now; he was in too deep.

'You did,' he added. 'I think you're very brave.' He knew he couldn't do it in his thirties, let alone at seventeen.

'Honestly, I wasn't brave enough for the alternatives. That really scared me. And so once it happened, I couldn't let him go. And that left me with only one alternative. To keep him.'

'Losing him would be worse?'

'Yes, without a doubt.'

He nodded and a funny taste formed in his mouth. He took a sip of water to wash it away. He felt like he was back on the cliff before abseiling. Or in the helicopter. Or at the bottom of that hill the day Joel died and he heard his dad's screams...

'Are you okay?' She stroked his hand with her thumb and he felt himself unravelling, so he turned away.

He wasn't okay, but he wasn't going to share this pain with her. He didn't want to share this sort of pain with anyone.

And that was why, as much as he wanted her, he could never be with Lucy.

CHAPTER SIXTEEN

EVERYTHING IS NORMAL. Everything is fine.

This was the mantra Lucy repeated to herself each morning on the way to work.

They had been back from Fiji for three days, three workdays…three mornings, lunchtimes, three departures, and Marcus had done no more than exchange superficial pleasantries as they passed each other in the office. She'd sent him work emails, and he'd sent polite replies.

Three days of nothing, Marcus keeping a deliberate distance, Lucy avoiding eye contact. Day by day, telling herself that this was what she wanted, while simultaneously nervous sickness was growing inside her. It felt like disappointment. Which was silly. They had agreed to a night of fun. He'd said he didn't regret what had happened, but they hadn't talked about seeing one another again. Maybe he was being more mature and sensible about this whole thing than she was and he knew that what happened in Fiji was best left in Fiji.

If she'd had more experience dating, she might have known what to do in this situation, but she hadn't and she didn't.

Saying he didn't regret anything had probably been his way of letting her down easily. Like saying *I'll call you* when he had no intention of actually calling.

What did you expect? That he'd serenade you in the office? That he'd change his mind about wanting children? That he'd become a different person?

'Thank you everyone. That's enough for now,' Marcus said to end the meeting. Then, as she was standing, he added, 'Lucy, do you have a moment?'

Lucy's heart paused. She nodded and hummed agreement. She was careful to wait until Marcus had closed the door behind the last of the others before she looked at him. Was he unhappy with her work? Had he decided she wasn't a good fit for the firm after all?

Marcus really wasn't ever going to settle down, have a family. His brother's death had affected him so profoundly, so deeply. He probably hadn't even begun to process it, not really. He was gunning for the big government campaigns. No smoking. Road safety. Of course! It all made sense now. The comment had seemed incongruous coming from the Marcus she thought she knew—ambitious, entrepreneurial. But that had been his aim all along. And the OZ Airways campaign was the way to prove his legitimacy, that he wasn't just a brash young thing. That he should be taken seriously.

'How are you doing?' he asked. His voice sounded strange. Awkward, even.

He was about to tell her that everything that had happened in Fiji had been a mistake.

'Fine,' she answered, hoping her voice was more steady than his.

'How often does Alex look after Lachie?'

'He's meant to pick him up from after-school care this afternoon.'

A slow, suggestive smile spread across Marcus's face.

'You probably have other plans, but I wanted to let you know that I don't. And I was planning on getting some dinner after work and I thought that if you don't have plans it might be something we could do together.'

'I don't,' she whispered.

'You don't have plans or you don't want to?'

'I don't have plans.'

The next couple of weeks Lucy felt like she was living someone else's life. When Lachie went to Alex, Lucy went to Marcus. When Lachie was tucked up in bed at her parents' house at night Lucy, with her mother's cheerful encouragement, met with Marcus. The guilt she felt at taking advantage of her parents' generosity, even though her mum insisted it was no problem at all, never went away…but her hunger for Marcus made voluntarily stopping seem simply unimaginable. For most of the week, she was Lucy Spencer, quiet achiever, Lachie's mum. At Marcus's apartment, wrapped in his arms, too busy staring into his eyes to enjoy the waterfront view, she was someone else entirely. Someone she'd never dreamed she could be. Someone impossible because they both knew this thing had an expiry date. They just didn't know when it was. Right now, they were all just focusing on the big pitch and every time Lucy thought about the slogan they had come up with she felt full of warmth and pride.

Australia—fall in love again.

When Marcus had raised it with the group, everyone had agreed it was the winning idea.

Lucy, though glad to have helped Marcus come up with it, was under no illusions that it meant anything at all.

But sometimes, when she had a quiet moment, she would toss those words over in her head.

Fall in love again...

But no one was falling in love, were they? Instead, they had spoken honestly about how there was no future between them.

But then, as he lay next to her and the lights sparkled on the water outside the window of his stunning apartment, doubt crept in.

You can't always see the most dangerous things. Like volcanic ash beyond the horizon. Saltwater crocs beneath the surface.

* * *

One morning, Lucy approached her mother with downcast eyes.

'Totally feel free to say no to this, but since you're going to be late to work tomorrow anyway for your appointment, I was wondering if you...'

Kate gave Lucy a sly smile. '...if I would drop Lachie at school tomorrow so you can have an, ahem, sleepover tonight?'

Lucy blushed furiously. 'Forget I said anything.'

'It'd be my pleasure, darling. You go out and enjoy yourself.'

Lucy nodded gratefully. Tried not to smile. 'I can't tell you how much I appreciate everything you do for me.'

'I love you very much Lucy. And I'm glad, very glad that you are finally getting out there.'

'But?'

'I didn't say "but".'

'Your tone implied it.'

'No "buts"—that must be your guilty conscience.'

'I've got nothing to feel guilty about.'

Kate Spencer smiled. 'That's right, you don't. You've been the most devoted mother to Lachie. And, I could not have wished for a better daughter.'

Lucy felt her face start to redden. This was a bit much for eight in the morning. 'Really, Mum.'

'Really. You know your father and I were disappointed you became pregnant. But we haven't been disappointed by anything you did after that. We're in awe of the way you've looked after Lachie, the way you got through university, and we are so impressed by how hard you've worked and now…to watch your career taking off. We're so incredibly proud. And we just hope that Marcus deserves you.'

'Mum, it's not… That is, it's early days and not…' She lowered her voice. 'It's not serious.' The words tasted like acid in her mouth.

'But he knows about Lachie?' Kate asked.

Lucy nodded.

'Good. I'm glad you're not lying any longer,' her mother said.

Lucy's stomach lurched. She was still lying to Marcus. Only this time the lie hurt more than ever. The secret was harder to keep, but it was more important than ever that she did.

Lucy loved Marcus. She loved him with her body and her soul. And she could never let him know.

CHAPTER SEVENTEEN

MUSICAL LAUGHTER FLOATED into Marcus's office and his chest clenched.

Traffic, telephones, printers and a hundred other sounds from the city, but the only thing he heard was Lucy's laughter. He glanced at the clock. It was nearly midday. He couldn't see her tonight, but maybe they could have lunch together. Maybe he could take her to a little restaurant he knew, discreet, out of the way. More discreet yet, maybe he could just order lunch to be delivered to his apartment...

The idea, once it occurred to him, could not be shifted.

We're five days out from the pitch—are you really going to take a long lunch? What is wrong with you?

He had to eat. And so did Lucy. What difference was an hour or two going to make at this stage?

Lucy was talking to Daphne outside his office, wearing a simple black shift dress. On anyone else it would have been an ordinary dress, but on Lucy it was transformed into a designer piece.

'Lucy? Can you pop in for a second and look at something for me?'

She nodded and Daphne disappeared down the corridor. Marcus motioned for Lucy to join him

behind his desk so she could see his screen. It was
open to the Oracle home page and she looked at
him blankly.

'Can I take you to lunch?' he whispered.

A gentle smile crossed her lips.

'Okay. Where are we going?'

'Not far. Meet me in the foyer at one?'

She nodded.

'Actually, let's make it twelve.'

She laughed and those beautiful musical notes
hit his chest like a bomb.

Just after twelve they stepped into the elevator and travelled down to the basement carpark,
where Marcus had left his car.

'Where are we going?'

'You'll see,' he promised.

They pulled up a minute later in front of Marcus's building.

'I thought we were going to eat.'

'We are. Delivery will be here in a minute.' He
showed her his phone with the app sharing the
driver was a minute away.

'We could have eaten in the office.'

'We could have, that's true. But you're the one
who's saying I need more work/life balance.'

She gave him a wry grin.

'Do you want to go straight back?' he asked.
Maybe he'd overstepped the line here. This was
business hours and he was her boss…but things

had been going so well. They were enjoying one another's company and they had an understanding. No pressure, no commitment.

'I didn't say that,' she murmured, and his heart sang.

A delivery driver arrived shortly afterwards with a bag of fresh gourmet sandwiches and salads. Marcus had chosen them specifically because they wouldn't go cold.

It was strange being in his apartment in the middle of the day; he was usually only home as the sun was rising and then only after it had set. The world looked different in this bright light. His apartment looked different with Lucy in it, unpacking the lunch.

'Leave it just a moment.' He stepped up behind her and wrapped her in his arms, breathing her in, savouring everything about her and this moment.

'I thought we were having lunch,' she giggled.

'We will. Eventually. I'm not going to send you back to the office hungry. Unsatisfied.'

Lucy shivered in his arms and her body melted into his. He ran his hands down her arms, over her hips and back up again, feeling her muscles relax and melt as he did. A gentle sigh escaped her lips and she spun to face him. His body came alight, pulsating, groaning, wanting her with every fibre of his being.

They made love on his living room floor, the sunlight streaming in and bathing her skin and hair in its golden light. His eyes never left her, wanting to see every moment, commit it to memory.

He didn't want to stop. He didn't want to leave this place. He didn't want to let her go.

CHAPTER EIGHTEEN

THREE DAYS OUT from the final presentation, Lucy was shocked by the amount of work that still needed to be done. They were close to being prepared and yet it didn't feel that way at all. They all knew so much was riding on this one presentation and none of them wanted to stop until it was perfect. Marcus had apologised as he'd asked some of the team to come into the office on a Saturday. The others had just shrugged, like they had expected it all along.

'Lucy, if you can't—' Marcus began.

'No, I can.' She cut him off. It was Alex's weekend. He had begged off taking Lachie on the Friday night because of 'clients.' Lucy had been disappointed, since that was one less night with Marcus, but she had capitulated because Alex would pick Lachie up on Saturday morning and she would be able to work on Saturday, just like everyone else. And she and Marcus would still have Saturday night…

At nine-fifteen on Saturday morning Alex still hadn't arrived. At nine-sixteen she called him.

'Hey,' he said when he finally picked up his phone.

'Are you far away?'

'Oh, yeah, I was going to call you.'

Dread curled up through her gut. 'What is it?'

'So it's Genevieve's sister's birthday and we're going to a winery. It's not exactly child friendly.'

'But you agreed. You know I have to work.'

'He can't make you work on a Saturday.'

'Excuse me?'

'Your hours are nine to five, weekdays. He can't make you work today.'

Anger surged through her. 'Are you serious?' She said loudly enough for Lachie to turn and look at her. She moved to the other room and closed the door. Her parents had gone away for the weekend, their first weekend away in who knew how long. They had offered to stay but Lucy had insisted; it wasn't fair that their life got put on hold because of her any longer. 'How many times have you worked overtime to further your career? How many weekends have you worked to get ahead or because the work needed doing?' she challenged Alex.

'That's different.'

'How is it different?'

Silence.

'Because you're the man?'

There was a long silence before he snapped, 'No need to overreact. I'll see if my parents can do it.'

'They'll have to.'

Lucy hung up and paced the room while she waited for either Alex or his parents to call back.

Three minutes later her phone buzzed. It was a text from Derick Rankin.

We have plans. Next time don't leave arranging such a thing to the last minute. We might be able to babysit him for an hour the Saturday after next.

Lucy's chest tightened with rage and her eyes stung with stubborn tears. She grabbed a tissue and angrily wiped her face.

No. She wasn't going to cry.

They couldn't even call her! Not Alex, not his father. She wanted to crawl into bed and howl.

But she'd never done that before and she wasn't about to now.

She pushed open the door and Lachie looked up at her.

'Guess what, sweetheart? You're going to be able to see where I work after all.'

Lucy didn't know what, if anything, Marcus said to the team. He had been overly polite when she'd called him. Using his best understanding-and-politically-correct-boss voice.

But no amount of understanding could assuage her mortification. Now everyone at work would know about Lachie. And they would know that she had lied.

Lachie loved getting the train into town and then going to 'Mummy's office.' He looked around in open-mouthed wonder as she led him behind the reception at Oracle and to the offices behind.

Daphne, Liam, everyone looked up with blank expressions when Lucy and Lachie walked in. She did her best to block out the looks of surprise and focused only on Marcus, which wasn't easier, but at least it was only one shocked look to deal with.

'I'm so sorry. Alex bailed, and then his parents. Mum and Dad are away and I'm jammed.'

'I told you, you didn't need to come in.'

'I'm not going to shirk my responsibilities, Marcus.'

'It's okay,' he said, jaw tight.

'He won't be a bother. He can sit in the kitchen. I've got his iPad and some books.'

'He can sit in my office if he likes, I've got a TV and a PlayStation.'

Lachie's eyes widened and looked from Marcus and then to Lucy. 'I want to work here when I grow up. Mum, can I work here when I'm grown up?'

Daphne and Liam giggled, but it did little to loosen the tension in the room.

'Really? A PlayStation?' Lucy asked.

Marcus shrugged. Grinned. 'It helps me to relax.'

'Lachie? Hi, I'm Marcus.' Marcus held out his hand, and Lucy's heart broke at the awkward and overly polite gesture. Lachie's eye widened and he looked to Lucy. She nodded her consent and Lachie took Marcus's hand.

'Let me show you my office.' Then Marcus looked at Lucy and she nodded again.

She tried to keep her heart rate steady and she watched Marcus lead Lachie to his office.

CHAPTER NINETEEN

'I'M SORRY,' Lucy said to him in the kitchen later that morning.

He hated she felt the need to keep apologising. 'I'm making you work on a Saturday. I'm the baddie here, not you.'

'You're not the baddie. Alex is the villain. And his father's possibly the devil.'

'They wouldn't take him?'

'No. When Alex bailed he asked his father if he could take Lachie and then his father sent me this charming text.'

She took her phone out. 'I need a reality check. Am I being overly sensitive? Or is this a horrible message?'

Marcus took the phone, read the text and passed it back to Lucy.

'It is a rude text,' he agreed, clenching his jaw. A father who didn't want to see his son. A grandfather who didn't jump at the chance to see his grandson. What would Marcus's father have done to see Joel again? To be a grandparent? It was a blessing, an honour. Not a chore.

Marcus knew in his heart that Lucy had never imposed, never asked more than what was her due. What should have been her right.

He felt the anger in his chest, in his throat. What kind of men were these?

'Lucy, that time you had to leave suddenly, that night in the pub. That was Alex cancelling, wasn't it?'

Lucy nodded.

Marcus knew he was hardly the poster boy for well-adjusted humans, but the attitude of these men shocked him. Lucy was not the one shirking her responsibilities. If anyone was irresponsible, it was Alex. And as for his father? If Derick Rankin had been in front of Marcus right now, he would have taken him by his collar and told him in no uncertain terms how ungrateful he was to have not just a living son but a grandson as well.

'Alex's father hates me.'

'Hates?' The man was clearly unhinged if he felt anything other than affection for Lucy Spencer.

'He thinks I ruined Alex's life and punishes me by refusing to see Lachie. He thinks he's teaching me a lesson about responsibility.'

'Sounds like he's only punishing Lachie.'

'Yes,' she agreed.

And it sounds like his son isn't very good at managing his own responsibilities, thought Marcus.

And they had the nerve to call Lucy irresponsible.

* * *

Lucy was in his office, giving Lachie the lunch she had prepared for him at home. Marcus sat at the table in the boardroom and reached for his phone. Swiped, found his mother's number.

Stop, you're being ridiculous. This is not your problem to solve. You're overstepping the mark so far you'll fall off the edge.

He couldn't ask his mother to help, even though he knew his mother would agree in a heartbeat. She loved children; she would adore Lachie. He was inquisitive, polite, with a touch of cheekiness.

Lachie had a thick mop of dark hair and big round, serious brown eyes, just like his mother's.

If Lachie were his son he wouldn't choose a winery over him. Hell, if Lachie were his grandson he wouldn't quibble over how much notice he'd been given. A kid wasn't an appointment—they didn't run to a timetable.

You'll never have a grandson since you'll never have a kid...

Marcus put his phone down and steadied himself with a few deep breaths. He was being ridiculous. It was the stress of the pitch. That was all. Lachie was fine watching TV and reading books in his office. They were all working together in the boardroom anyway.

Lachie was fine.

And it was none of *his* business.

Marcus tasted salt. He stood and left the room. He had to stop thinking about his brother. He couldn't think of his father. Or of his mother, who would cut out her own kidneys for a grandkid.

His mother, who never would be a grandparent. Who had lost a son and then a husband and now…?

Oh, damn, he was a mess. He had to get a grip.

Marcus ordered in some Turkish pizzas and salads for lunch and they all ate at their desks. Around about 2:00 p.m. Lucy started stretching more than usual.

'Marcus, do you mind if I take a quick walk around outside? I'm starting to get a bit stiff. I think Lachie could do with a bit of fresh air. We won't be long. I'll just take him for a run around the gardens.'

'Of course,' he said thinking that it was probably a good idea.

Lucy glanced over his shoulder at his laptop, where the pitch was open in front of him. He had been working on this line for nearly two hours and couldn't get it right.

Lucy disappeared in the direction of his office and a few minutes later came back with her jacket on and Lachie by the hand. 'Can Marcus come too?' he asked.

Marcus's eyes found Lucy's and she looked stricken. 'Lachie, honey, Marcus is very busy.'

He wasn't getting anywhere with this line and was going to be working late tonight as it was. A walk outside while the sun was still out wouldn't hurt.

'I might just do that.' He stood, stretched his arms towards the ceiling and heard something in his neck crack as he saw a grin cross over Daphne's face. Both Daphne and Liam had picked up on his connection with Lucy, but given they were also conducting a secret relationship, they were all being very discreet with one another.

'You don't have to, really,' Lucy said.

'No, it's fine. Come on, Lachie, show me the gardens. I haven't been in years.'

Lachie's already big eyes opened even wider. 'But your office is right across the road!'

The grin was still on Lucy's face but she was looking at the floor.

'Well, I have a great view of them. I look at them every day—just because I don't go and walk through them I still enjoy them.'

Lachie wasn't convinced by this explanation. 'But you don't get ice cream.'

Marcus stifled a laugh. 'No, it's true. I don't get ice cream.'

Lachie held out his hand. 'Come on, Marcus, I'll show you.'

Marcus saw Daphne trying not to smile and focusing very determinedly on her screen.

Lachie wanted to cross the road directly in front of the building, but Marcus insisted on walking fifteen metres up to the nearest pedestrian crossing. Lachie didn't want to hold his mother's hand, but Marcus stood close enough to grab him if necessary as they crossed the busy six-lane road. Once they were across the road and through the gates of the Botanic Garden, Marcus relaxed a bit and let Lachie lead the way. He followed Lachie up over the hill and then down, through the fernery, to the Lotus Pond and down to the harbour's edge. Marcus couldn't remember the last time he'd walked through the gardens, even though they were literally on both his office's and apartment's doorstep.

You could detour through here every morning and night on your way to and from the office, adding no more than ten minutes to your trip.

Had he been so wrapped up in his own stuff he couldn't see the treasure that was literally in front of him?

Yes. He had.

They looped around the edge of the harbour. It was a crisp, clear winter day. The sun danced on the water and the sky was as blue as it could be. Lucy answered all of Lachie's questions as they went, while Marcus walked a few feet back and watched. A slight breeze lifted off the water, bringing with it the smell of spring. It blew Lucy's hair around her face and took his own breath away.

She tipped her head back and laughed at something Lachie had said and hit him in the chest. It was the most beautiful thing he'd ever seen.

Is this what love felt like? This feeling of wanting to be close to this woman always, to never want to stop looking at her?

No. That was just lust, surely.

Besides, those feelings for Lucy came with unpleasant ones: the feeling he got when Lachie got too close to the water's edge. Or didn't look three times before crossing the busy road. Those feelings. The way his muscles seized. The way his throat went dry. The way his heart rate rocketed so fast he felt faint. Those feelings weren't pleasant at all. Those were feelings he was not cut out for.

But it was okay; Lucy knew where they stood and she didn't want a relationship any more than he did. They were keeping things casual. Because that's all it could ever be.

'Ice cream!' Lachie screamed and grabbed the nearest hand, which happened to be Marcus's. He dragged Marcus to the van and pointed to the largest ice cream on offer, the one that was also covered in the most confectionary.

'Hang on, we'd better ask your mum.'

Lachie let out an exaggerated groan. Lucy caught up with them and shook her head when she saw Lachie's selection.

'One of those, please.' Lucy pointed at a smaller chocolate-covered cone. 'Do you want something?' she asked Marcus.

He was about to shake his head following his first instinct. Why would he eat an ice cream on a Saturday afternoon? But the smell of melted chocolate hit his nostrils and he began to salivate.

'I'll get it.' He nodded and ordered two more chocolate-covered cones. The three of them licked their ice creams as they walked back up the hill.

Marcus was looking at the biggest, most impressive kangaroo paw flower he'd ever seen when the final line of the pitch just came to him. Like a flash from nowhere. Lucy and Lachie were counting some nearby ducks and he took out his phone to write it down before he forgot it. He looked back to Lucy and Lachie, who were now pretending to walk like ducks. A deep sense of satisfaction and relief washed through his tight, aching body.

When they returned from the gardens, Marcus went back to work on the presentation. For the first time all day he had that excited, energetic feeling he sometimes got when he knew in his bones that what he was focused on worked. He was immersed in his work all afternoon, so absorbed he hardly noticed as the light faded outside. Someone ordered dinner at some stage and finally, around 9:00 p.m, he pushed his chair back put his hands behind his head and stretched. They were done. And it was perfect.

'I'm glad we pushed through,' Lucy said, next to him. She rubbed her eyes and he realised suddenly how late it was. She was still here. And so, he assumed, must Lachie be.

'Is it okay if I head off home now?' Lucy asked him and the sense of satisfaction he'd felt moments ago was now slightly soured.

'Of course. You should have left ages ago.'

'I wanted to do my share,' she insisted.

Marcus looked around the boardroom and focused on everyone properly for the first time in hours. Daphne was clearing away all the drafts, and Liam was tidying up the remains of the dinner. Lachie was fast asleep on the couch in the corner. He should've told Lucy to leave earlier.

'How are you getting home?' he asked.

She shrugged. 'Train, I guess.'

He really was an insensitive jerk. 'No, you can't get the train—it's nine o'clock on a Saturday night. I'll pay for a cab.' As soon as he said those words he knew he sounded like an even bigger jerk. 'Actually, no, I'll drive you both.'

Lucy looked around the room, appearing to judge the others' reactions. But Daphne and Liam had both left the room. 'Marcus, it's okay. You don't have to.'

'I know, but it really is the very least I can do as…' He stopped the sentence there. What was he going to say? *As your boss*? *As your boyfriend*? 'I'm driving and that's that. My car's downstairs.'

'If you're sure. We've already been a bother today.'

'Are you kidding? I've made you work all Saturday. I can drive you home.'

She nodded and gathered her things. When they were ready to go, she roused Lachie by shaking him gently and whispering, 'Come on, it's time to go. Marcus is going to drive us home.'

Lachie lifted his head and opened his eyes wide. 'We're going with Marcus?'

'Yes, so you need to be on your best behaviour.'

Lachie scrambled up and the three of them caught the elevator down to the basement and his car.

'Wow!' Lachie exclaimed. 'Is that a Tesla?'

'You know your cars?'

'My dad told me. He's always wanted one of these,' Lachie said. 'I can't wait to tell him I got to drive in one.'

Marcus stole a look over to Lucy and even under the dim light to the basement could see her cheeks colour.

She was jittery. He could feel her anxiety from the other side of the car. She hadn't been this awkward the last time she'd driven in his car. The memory of their lunchtime tryst rocked through his veins, and the tiredness he felt moments ago was completely forgotten. But not tonight. Tonight she would go home with Lachie and he would go back to his empty, cold apartment.

Marcus unlocked the car and Lucy opened a back door for Lachie, who scrambled in.

Lucy slid into the front seat and he couldn't help watching her as she did so. It was a pity Lachie was here. Or it was just as well Lachie was here; otherwise he didn't think he'd be able to keep his hands to himself.

Lucy gave him directions. As they drove over the bridge, she turned to check on Lachie and whispered, 'Oh, he's gone to sleep.' A few moments later she continued, 'I'm so sorry again about today.'

'You don't have anything to be sorry about. I'm the one who asked you to work on a Saturday. His father was the one who bailed. His grandparents are the difficult ones. You, Lucy, you have absolutely nothing to be sorry for.' His mouth tasted odd as he spoke. He hated that she felt like this. He hated that this was the way she'd been taught to feel. As though everything the world gave her was a favour. That she was not entitled to ask for anything. To want anything.

'I should've been able to make other arrangements.'

'Your employer should not have expected you to work on a Saturday. Especially not to nine o'clock at night. I hope you manage to get some rest tomorrow. You need to be all refreshed for Monday.'

Lucy's head spun to look at him. 'Monday? You want me to come? To the presentation?'

'Of course I do, Lucy. You've been integral to the whole thing.' He didn't want to do the presentation without her. He didn't, he realised, want to do anything without her.

He glanced across at her and saw she was looking out the window. Her soft hands were in her lap, her fingers twisting together. 'Thank you,' she said. 'That means a lot to me.'

They drove in silence a while longer, the streets nearly empty, colourful lights sparkling everywhere.

'I'm sorry, Marcus, I've just realised. I meant to get some milk on the way home. There's a small shopping centre just near my house—it should still be open. Would you mind?'

'Of course not. Just show me the way.'

They pulled up to a small suburban mall, still bright and busy with several customers leaving with grocery bags.

'I don't usually go shopping so late,' she said.

He laughed. 'I do,' he said. He was usually one of those people ducking into the supermarket five minutes before it closed to buy something to make a late dinner with.

Lucy looked to the back seat where Lachie was sleeping peacefully. 'Do you mind just waiting here with him? I won't be long and I'm sure he'll just sleep.'

'Lucy, it's fine. Please, just go.'

Lucy closed the door as quietly she could behind her and rushed off into the shopping centre. Marcus watched her until she was inside, her gorgeous brown hair swishing behind her, pulling her jacket tight around herself to protect her from the cold evening air. He imagined her entering the supermarket, gathering what she needed. Was there ever a time when part of his thoughts were not on Lucy? On where she was, what she was doing, thinking, feeling? He sighed, realised he was smiling. Smiling like a lunatic for no other reason than he was thinking about her.

From the back seat a sleepy little voice called out, 'Mum?'

He turned. 'It's okay Mate, she's just ducked into the shops. She won't be long.'

'I need to go to the bathroom. I really need to go.'

Marcus's heart fell. He had no idea how long Lucy would be or even how far away they were from her house.

'Can you hold on a few minutes?'

'I don't think I can.'

Marcus sighed. Somewhere inside the small shopping centre would be a bathroom. 'Okay, come with me,' he said.

Marcus scanned the area; there were a few cars entering and leaving the car park. Should he take Lachie's hand? Could he watch for cars himself? Marcus walked next to Lachie, within grabbing distance, but didn't take his hand.

Get a grip! This is a suburban shopping centre—it'll be fine. They entered the brightly lit complex and Marcus scanned for signs to the toilets, while also keeping a watch over Lachie. When this proved impossible, he placed a hand on Lachie's shoulders and then looked for directions. Thankfully he saw the sign with the male figure and headed towards it.

They went to the bathroom and Marcus watched, without watching, as Lachie went. Lachie pulled up his pants and made to leave, but Marcus nodded to the sink and Lachie gave him a sly smile as if to indicate he was caught trying to get out of this last step. As Lachie washed his hands the door flung open hard and fast, banging hard against the wall, and an obviously inebriated, possibly high man followed quickly afterwards. Marcus moved swiftly between Lachie and the drunk.

'Whatcha staring at?' the man growled.

'Nothing, just leaving.'

With a hand on Lachie and his body in between Lachie and the drunk, Marcus steered Lachie out of the bathrooms, his heart racing and his hands suddenly clammy. Once they were well away from the bathrooms, he bent down and checked on Lachie.

'Are you okay?'

'What was wrong with him?' Lachie asked, wide-eyed and more excited than worried.

They saw Lucy coming out of the supermarket and Lachie ran to her. Marcus scanned the area again for other hazards and drunks. With nothing and no one around, he walked over to Lucy. Lachie was already telling her.

'What happened?' Lucy looked to Marcus for confirmation.

'Aggressive drunk in the bathroom.'

Lucy opened her eyes wide. Just like her son. 'Are you okay?'

'Lachie's fine.'

'I know he's fine Are you all right?'

Marcus nodded. He was the grown-up; of course he was okay. Even though his limbs still felt shaky. 'I'm just going to tell the security guard over there. Why don't you take Lachie to the car?' He handed her his keys.

The guard was also not perturbed. 'Happens all the time, mate. We'll shift him on.'

Was Marcus the only one worried? The man hadn't threatened them exactly, but he was unsteady, unstable and looked like he could blow at any moment.

Was Lucy always so relaxed around Lachie? Or was it something you learnt? Or was it simply because she'd never had to confront the sight of Lachie, bloody and lifeless by the side of the road. The memory that he'd been trying all day not to think about was suddenly front and centre of his mind. As unwelcome and frightening as always. Only this time, the body wasn't Joel's.

It was Lachie's.

Lucy's parents' place was only a street away. Marcus parked and walked them to the door. Lachie hung around at the door, telling Marcus again what a good time he'd had at Mummy's work and at the gardens. 'Go on in, sweetheart,' Lucy said, but Lachie didn't go.

It was probably just as well. A moment of privacy might lead to something that they wouldn't be able to finish, and Marcus was already drawn tightly enough as it was. The stress of the day, of the pitch. Of Lucy.

And Lachie. There was a scratching in his chest that he couldn't place, but couldn't shift either.

'Good night, Marcus. Thanks again for the lift.'

He nodded. 'Thank you for giving up your Saturday. See you on Monday.'

Her lips mouthed a perfect O. He was no lip reader but it looked like a kiss.

As he drove away, the memory of Lucy blowing him a kiss stayed with him. He wished he wasn't leaving her and going home alone to his cold apartment.

It wouldn't do.

Thinking about Lucy, being so distracted by her, had lost them so much time. If he hadn't wasted so much time yesterday, none of them would have had to work so late today. Lucy was not the plan. Lucy was a distraction. The fear he felt when he was around Lachie was a distraction And he didn't know what he was going to do about it.

He had to end it; it was the only way to stop the fear that he would lose her.

But by ending it, he would lose her anyway. And the thought of breaking up with her? That was too painful to contemplate.

What was he going to do?

CHAPTER TWENTY

UNLIKE THE DISASTER of Saturday morning, Monday morning flowed as smoothly as a full river. Lucy woke five minutes before her alarm was due to sound, having slept a long, deep, refreshing sleep. Lachie dressed himself and got ready for school without being reminded about anything. He kissed her goodbye and waved her off easily as Lucy left to catch the train. Her parents had arrived home as planned on Sunday afternoon, and her mother was going to take Lachie to school and pick him up from after-school care as well. Lucy had spent Sunday relaxing and doing some shopping and washing, getting ready for the week. She chose her outfit and laid it out the night before. She hadn't even spilled anything on it while eating her breakfast.

She arrived at work early, before most of the team, and even had time to get a coffee and go over her short presentation before they all got a cab down to the OZ Airways headquarters for the nine-o'clock meeting. She was extremely glad they were getting the presentation over and done with first thing. It would've been horrible to have to wait until later in the day as the knots in her stomach grew tighter and tighter. She glanced at Marcus, sitting in the front passenger seat of the taxi. He exuded calm and confidence; he was upbeat, joking with the others, but Lucy noticed the little things. He was swallowing more often than usual. His eyes just slightly red at the edges and his skin tone was just a little off. But maybe that was just the light in the cab.

No. He's anxious about something.

He's about to do one of the most significant presentations of his life, so of course he's looking a bit green. A bit tired.

But when Daphne asked him how he was feeling about the presentation, Marcus just smiled broadly and said he'd never felt so confident about a pitch in his entire life. 'And you know,' Marcus continued, 'if we don't get this account, I'm absolutely sure it won't be because of anything we did and didn't do. OZ will be the one missing out if they don't choose us.'

So, if he wasn't anxious about the presentation that currently had her heart rate rattling in her ears, what was wrong?

It couldn't be something to do with her, could it? Marcus probably had heaps of things going on in his high-powered life that had absolutely nothing to do with her.

He's been working like a machine since the Fiji trip. What else do you think he's possibly got time for? Apart from work, you have been his life.

They hadn't been alone since their lunchtime tryst last week. They hadn't even spoken about it.

She didn't know if that was normal. Did people who sneaked out for a 'long lunch' at their boss's apartment usually talk about it afterwards? She had no idea.

And Lachie had been with her all day on Saturday.

Although Marcus had told her over and over again that he wasn't upset she had to bring Lachie in with her to the office on the weekend, she couldn't help but think something had definitely shifted between them. Marcus had been so strange late Saturday night after that incident with the drunk at the shops. Overly worried. Weirdly anxious. Almost as though there was something about the incident he wasn't telling her.

She'd ask him after the pitch. Now wasn't the time. Certainly not when he was swallowing so much and when his skin had turned a slight shade of green.

If something terribly bad had happened, she needed to know. But she also knew, without a doubt, that if Lachie had been hurt, Marcus would have told her. And Lachie was fine, so what had happened? Maybe it wasn't the incident at the shops after all—maybe it was something else? Maybe it was simply the fact that she'd had to bring her kid into the office with her?

Marcus had been kind and accommodating to Lachie and had not blamed Lucy on Saturday.

No. That wasn't it exactly.

But Lucy knew what it was.

It was Lachie. Meeting him, spending time with him, seeing him as a real person and not just an idea.

While Lachie was still a theoretical concept, he could whisk Lucy away for lunchtime meetings. They could both pretend that she was carefree and unattached and the type of person who could just drop everything for a few hours to be pleasured and cherished by the man of her dreams.

It had been wonderful and thrilling, not just because Marcus made her feel things she never had before, but because for two glorious hours she'd felt like another person. She'd been given the opportunity to pretend that her life wasn't a frantic mix of work, Lachie, washing, cooking, trying to make it everywhere on time.

And that was just the problem right there.

She had been pretending to be someone else. First by lying about Lachie. Then escaping reality in Fiji. And then by meeting her boss for a lunchtime assignation. None of those things were her real life.

Marcus had made an effort with Lachie because Lucy was his employee. But when it came to the other side of their relationship, Lachie was an impediment. A barrier.

Now it was Lucy's turn to swallow several times in quick succession. Her skin was probably also looking a bit peaky too by the time they pulled up at the OZ offices. It hit her as the cab pulled over and she slid along the back seat to climb out onto the curb.

It couldn't happen again.

Not the lunchtime antics. Not the Saturdays in the office. None of it.

She'd known all along it could never work with Marcus. She'd suspected it on her first day at Oracle. And she'd known it in Fiji, from their very first kiss on the beach.

She'd known it when he'd told her that he didn't want a family. She'd known but she'd been pretending otherwise. This thing was Marcus was wonderful, amazing, head spinning, earth shifting. But it was all a lie. She'd been pretending all along.

And she'd been lying to herself about the biggest thing. She'd fooled herself into believing that her heart was safe. That she could handle her feelings for Marcus and set them to one side when the time came.

That was the biggest lie of all.

As she watched him give the presentation of his life, Lucy knew that Marcus Hawke was a man she would never be able to get over. She would never meet another man who would come close to satisfying her physically or intellectually or emotionally. He was the only man she would ever want. And the one she could never have.

* * *

She typed the email of resignation when they arrived back from the pitch. There was no point lingering over it; that would just make things worse. She hit Send on the message and began to finish off the last of her projects.

It was moments later that her phone rang. Marcus. Her heart pounded in her throat as she picked up the receiver.

'Hello.'

'Lucy.' His voice was rough. Strained. 'Can I see you in my office?'

'I'm not sure.'

'We're not having this conversation over the phone. Please come in here immediately. Or I'll have to come out onto the floor.'

He had her there. Going into Marcus's office at this point was about as appealing as a root canal, but having him come out and discuss her resignation in front of everyone? That was as appealing as a root canal with no anaesthetic.

Her legs somehow carried her into his office. She closed the door behind her before she dared look at his face.

'What's this about?'

'You know what it's about.'

He narrowed his eyes. 'You really want to leave Oracle?'

She didn't want to, but she had to. Her future depended on it.

'I think it would be for the best.'

'Are you sure? Absolutely sure?'

The only thing she was sure of was that it would hurt less to break up now. 'It's easier this way.'

His eyes drew narrower.

He wasn't begging her to stay with him; he was only asking her not to resign.

You were right. He has been thinking about ending your relationship since he met Lachie.

'Lucy, we agreed…this thing between us, it won't affect our work. And it won't affect your job.'

'Marcus, please be realistic.'

'I am. Lucy, you're great in this job. You have something special. Please don't resign.'

I have to. Don't you see? I can't be in the same room as you without simultaneously wanting to take your clothes off and sob with heartbreak at the same time.

'I love working here. The opportunity to work with you has been an honour. But you know as well as I do that this firm isn't the best fit for a single mother.'

'I can make it be.'

She shook her head. 'I'm not asking you to do that. I get how the business works. I get how you work—full steam ahead, inspiration can strike at all hours, all the deadlines. And that's okay. Maybe one day, when Lachie is older, I'll be able to take on a job like this, but for the next few years, it isn't where I need to be.'

'The last few weeks have been the exception. It isn't usually like this. And when it is, I will help you. We can arrange care for Lachie. We can have him in here.'

She shook her head. 'It isn't just that. It's every day. Every single day I feel like I'm letting the team down when I leave at five. Every day I worry that something will be wrong with the trains and I won't get to Lachie in time. Every. Single. Day. And that's not your fault—that's life. It was my decision to have him—I have to deal with this.'

'I'll make changes around here. Flexible work arrangements. You can work from home if you like, I'll give more carers' leave. School holiday leave.'

'That's great, but the next parent you hire can use those.'

'Why not you?'

Because I love you, don't you see? 'Because this isn't just about better conditions.'

'Then what is it about?'

You have to tell him. You can't expect him to just know.

Can't I? Can't he figure this out? Doesn't he see that I'm in love with him?

'This isn't easy for me, none of it. Please respect my decision,' she said with difficulty.

Lucy was sure that somewhere in that conversation she had broken up with him. But they hadn't really discussed *that* at all; they had mostly talked about her job and how he didn't want her to resign.

Did their relationship really mean so little to him that he didn't even care to argue with her about it?

You didn't have a relationship. You had a fling.

Then this really was all for the best.

'I'm not happy about this.'

'Marcus, I'm not thrilled about any of it either. But it's for the best.'

She hoped he left it at that. While it hurt that he'd rather fight for her job then their relationship, she knew she should be grateful. She didn't want to have to spend too long convincing him that they should stop seeing each other. She couldn't tell him the real reason they had to end things. She couldn't confess to the fact that she'd gone and lost her heart to him. That she had to end things to protect herself. And Lachie.

'What about us?' He spoke quietly, almost as though he didn't want her to hear.

'Can't you see this...' She waved her hands between them. If she couldn't even say 'us' aloud, how was she going to tell him that she had fallen in love with him?

They were meant to keep things casual— falling in love wasn't part of the deal.

She had lied to him again, but not anymore. She had to have the courage to tell the truth. And to ask for what she wanted. She was worth it.

The words came out in a whoosh and once the dam was open the words kept coming.

'I've fallen in love with you, Marcus. I didn't mean to, but I did. I was probably a bit in love with you all along. I was lying to you about that too. Lying to myself that I didn't want anything serious. But no more.'

Marcus buried his face in his palms. When he looked up his eyes were red, but dry.

'I'm sorry, Lucy.'

'I know.

'I could fall for you.'

She touched his arm. 'But you haven't.'

'It's so soon and it's been a busy, stressful time.'

'And you know as well as I do that when we win the account, which we will, it's only going to get busier. And I'm not going to force it. I tried that once and it didn't work. Your work, your drive, it's part of who you are. I understand why and I would never ask you to jeopardise your career in any way. I get why you need to do what you do and I love you too much to ever ask you to change. You are devoted to your career and I'm devoted to Lachie.'

'Lucy—'

'Marcus, please don't make it any harder than it already is. We both know we'd just be delaying the inevitable.'

He sighed, deep, long and resigned. 'You're the most amazing woman I've ever known. I need you to know that.'

One side of her mouth twitched into a smile. 'I don't blame you, not a little bit. This is about me having the confidence to ask for what I want. For what I need.'

She nodded. It was the only form of communication she trusted her body to make.

She didn't remember turning, or walking across the thick carpeted floor of his office and out to her cubicle. She didn't remember turning off her computer. She was only vaguely aware of walking out through the foyer and catching the lift to the ground floor.

Out on the street the rest of the city was oblivious to what had just happened. And that was probably a good thing. She felt as though her heartbreak was written right across her face.

On the train home she stared blankly out the window. She had done the right thing. She had absolutely done the right thing. Marcus didn't love her and so there was no point hanging around and torturing herself. She deserved more than casual. She deserved everything. She wasn't foolish or irresponsible. She was mature beyond her years, talented and hardworking. And she had so much love to give.

She was worthy of someone who felt the same way about her as she did about them.

Leaving Marcus was the most grown-up thing she'd ever done. And she just wanted to cry in her mother's arms.

CHAPTER TWENTY-ONE

HE THOUGHT IT would feel different to this. Sure, he was satisfied. Proud. And he could even get caught up in the euphoric mood of the office as he shouted them all drinks the night OZ Airways rang to tell him that Oracle Creative had won the account.

He was satisfied, but he wasn't happy.

He stared at his phone, sitting on the table next to a half-drunk glass of flat champagne. He could text her. He had news. No, he *should* text her, to let her know they had won.

Hi, just thought you'd want to know that we won the OZ account. We couldn't have done it without you, M x

He hit Send. Then instantly wondered if he'd said the right thing. Should he have said more? Less? Invited her to celebrate with them?

No. He'd said just enough. She didn't want to see him; she'd made it clear that seeing him would only make things harder for her and he was determined to respect that. It was the least he could do for her.

Her reply came over an hour later. They were

still at the bar and he was wondering if the last champagne he'd drunk had been a bad idea.

That's fantastic! Congratulations! I'm so pleased, though I didn't doubt it for a second. Lucy xx

Even though her message was upbeat, it left him flat. There was no longer any reason to write back. Winning the pitch was the grand extent of his news.

It was big news, to be sure, but it was also all he had to say. It was the only thing going on in his life.

I'm miserable. I miss you.

That wasn't news and she didn't need to know it.

She was probably miserable too, but she had the good sense to realise that telling him about it wouldn't help.

It would only delay the inevitable.

She was right; he was committed to his career and she was committed to Lachie. She knew how important his job was and would never ask him to change his life for her.

But what if he wanted to change his life?

No. This was the champagne talking. And exhaustion. Winning the OZ account wasn't the pinnacle of his career; it was the beginning of the upward trajectory. Everything he'd been working for all his life.

Besides, there was Lachie. He couldn't let himself be put in any kind of caring position for Lachie. Gorgeous, clever, cheeky Lachie. Just thinking about him brought his big brown eyes to Marcus's mind. There was no way he could get to know Lachie, get to care for him. And certainly not any other children...

He took another swig of champagne and his head spun. He put his glass down again. There was no point writing himself off tonight; the real work started tomorrow.

On Saturday he went to his mother's for lunch. It had been a few weeks since he'd seen her, between the visit to Fiji, working on the pitch. And Lucy. They sat on her balcony and soaked up the spring sunshine as they ate the creamy chicken pie she'd prepared.

'How did you go with that woman?' Veronica asked once he was halfway through his meal.

'What woman?' he asked. Though he sensed he knew, he hoped she was talking about something else.

'The one you were worried about. The one you thought might have an abusive partner.'

'She didn't—she's fine.'

'Oh, good, I'm glad to hear that. But did you ever find out what's going in her life?'

She had no idea what she was getting into but he found it hard to keep his expression composed.

'Yes, she has a son. That was all.'

'A son? Really? That's a relief.'

It was, and it also wasn't. He kept eating his pie.

'I suppose she just told you?'

'Something like that.'

'And how's she doing? Being a mother and coping with the Oracle culture?'

He put his fork down. He may as well just come out with it, since she would chip away at him with her benign questions until it all came out anyway.

'She resigned, a week ago. But not because of the workload. Well, maybe that too. But mostly because of me.'

Veronica's eyebrows came together in a concerned furrow.

'We started seeing one another.'

'I see.'

'And we were keeping things casual.'

'Of course you were.'

He caught a hint of condescension in her tone. 'But she, well, she began to develop feelings for me.'

'Feelings! My, my…not *feelings*.'

'Mum,' he warned. He expected a lecture on sleeping with his staff. Or leading someone on.

Instead she simply said, 'Tell me about her.'

And that was a harder question to answer. 'Her name's Lucy, she's twenty-three and probably the most talented designer I've come across in years.

She's clever, gorgeous and altogether wonderful. And she has a five-year-old son, Lachie.'

'Five years old? But she must have been—'

'She got pregnant when she was seventeen. She somehow managed to finish school and then university while raising him. Her parents help, though I don't think Lachie's father does much.'

'She sounds amazing.'

He nodded. 'She is.' *The most amazing woman I've ever met.*

'But you don't have feelings for her?'

'Our lives aren't compatible.' He hadn't answered his mother's question and he didn't care.

'How are they not? You're young and single—she's young and single.'

'I have a business.'

'Marcus, work is your life. And maybe there's nothing wrong with that. If it really is what you want. But if you're using work as a crutch or an excuse to avoid other things, then that may not be the best thing in the long run. You're driven, and you're focused, but you're also immature.'

'Immature? That's a bit brutal.' He was trying to help people, build a better world. How could his own mother not see that?

'Maybe, but it's what you need to hear.'

'I run a successful business. I've just won the account to design the biggest ad campaign of the year. How can I be immature?'

She studied him, cocked her head. He didn't

like how that look made him feel. Foolish. Stupid. *Immature*.

'Mum, she has a kid. It'd be wrong of me to get involved with her when I have no intention of having a family.'

'Don't you want a family? One day?'

Her words crushed his heart. But not as much as he would be crushing hers to confirm the truth. He didn't want a family. He didn't want children. He didn't want to subject either of them to that kind or worry, that kind of pain.

'I think it's for the best, don't you?'

The look on her face told him, no, she didn't agree. Not one bit. 'Do you think you can just go through life without being hurt? Without pain? You can try, but you won't live much of a life.'

'If you'd have known what was going to happen to Joel and Dad, you wouldn't have married Dad or had Joel.'

She laughed. 'Of course I would have. I would never have not loved your father. I have a lot of regrets, but marrying your father and having Joel are still definitely two of the greatest things I've ever done. Besides, if I hadn't had a first son, how could I have had a second?' She reached over and squeezed his hand. Marcus stared at the table.

'But how? How can I love someone when it could be taken away at any moment?'

'That knowledge just makes it more important to cherish the moments you do have. Marcus, darling, I'm so sorry, I had no idea you felt like this. I was so consumed with your father, I didn't realise you were going through this. You always seemed so…well, not fine, exactly. But coping.'

'I've been coping.'

'You've been coping by refusing to let yourself feel—that's not the same thing. You're lucky, though. You're young…it isn't too late to give me grandchildren.' She smiled and brushed away an errant tear.

Maybe not. But it was too late to win Lucy.

CHAPTER TWENTY-TWO

IT WAS GOOD being back working for her old firm, Birdseye Design. It was a nice, relaxed firm, close to home and Lachie's school. And her new boss, Henry, who was actually her old boss, was sixty years old and very happily married with his second grandchild on the way. She didn't need a big fancy firm in the CBD; everything she needed in a career was right here. Henry had also offered her extremely flexible arrangements. He didn't care if she worked from the office, home or a cafe; as long as she turned her designs in on time, he was happy. And Lucy was too.

She was sad about Marcus, but she was resigned to that sadness. She accepted it and got on with things. Strangely, she'd never felt stronger. Or more confident. She'd refused to back down when Alex had yet again tried to get out of looking after Lachie and asked him, right in front of his girlfriend, what kind of father shirked his responsibilities like that? The look on Alex's girlfriend's face had been priceless.

As for Derick Rankin, Lucy decided not to care any longer. He could say what he liked, but Lachie grew up seeing the truth every day, how his mother loved him and devoted her life to him and one day, probably not even far from now, Lachie would realise what a dinosaur his paternal grandfather was.

Lucy may not have a boyfriend, but she decided she was going to have girlfriends. She had reconnected with an old friend from school, who was now expecting her first baby. She also had plans to go out this Friday night with some women she had been friendly with at uni, though she'd never had the chance to really socialise with them.

She might be sad, but life was still good.

She was finishing the proofs of a new account for Henry when her phone pinged with a message. She swiped it open and read:

I thought you might want to be one of the first to see the final product. M x.

There was a link that took her to a video. She saw at once it was the completed advertisement. Her logo, her font were the same.

The clip opened with a young couple, gorgeous and in love, walking hand in hand along a pristine beach.

'Australia, fall in love…' said the voice over.

This was what they had planned; it gave her tingles to see it complete. The next scene was meant to be the same couple at Uluru and then travelling all over the country. But then, instead of the young couple in the outback, there was a shot of the same couple, now with the woman visibly pregnant and walking with her partner in Sydney, near the Opera House. In the next shot, the couple were with a toddler and exploring a rainforest, and in the next they were with two young kids, one about Lachie's age, camping at Uluru. The film went on and the couple and the children aged until, in the penultimate shot, the couple were surrounded by two other couples, their grown children and young children. The ad faded out with an old couple walking along the first beach. 'Australia, fall in love again, and again and again.'

The phone shook in Lucy's hands and she sniffed. The image on her phone became blurry. She took some deep breaths and brushed away the tears pooling in her eyes.

'OZ Airways, let us take you home.'

Lucy put down her phone and turned back to her computer.

Five minutes later she hit Submit on a draft design for her boss, glad that was the last major thing she had to do all week. She wasn't sure she'd be able to concentrate on anything else right now. He'd changed the script.

He'd changed it and made it better...

But why? And why send it to her when it wasn't the script she'd worked on?

She read the message over and over again, even though she already knew it by heart.

It was just before twelve thirty. She could take a lunchbreak. Everyone else here did. Besides, it was a perfect spring day, bright and clear but not too hot. A walk would do her good. She picked up her bag and left. Her new office was a quick train ride from the Oracle offices, and her feet, knowing what she hadn't yet accepted herself, walked towards the eastern edge of town.

She had entered the building and called the elevator before she knew what she was going to say and arrived in the Oracle foyer before she'd even come up with a plausible reason for being there. She'd left something behind.

No. She was Lucy Spencer, designer, mother, and she didn't make excuses anymore.

Then why was she there? She wasn't sure she knew. To casually drop by and congratulate him?

It was Tara who saw her first, for which she was grateful. There was no reason to lie to Tara. She beamed when she saw Lucy. 'Couldn't stay away—I knew it.'

'No, I've just… That is, would it be possible to grab five minutes with Marcus? I'll wait—it won't take long.'

She couldn't tell Tara why she needed to see Marcus, since she had no idea herself. She didn't have the first clue what she was going to say, only that she somehow needed to know why he'd changed the script. Or that she sensed there was something he wanted to say to her.

'No can do,' Tara quipped, and Lucy's heart plummeted. 'He isn't here.'

'Oh, do you know when he'll be back?'

'Not until tomorrow. It's his day off.'

'His what?'

I haven't taken a day off in years.

Marcus just didn't do days off.

'His day off,' Tara repeated. 'That's what we all do now. Four-day weeks. He still pays us the same, but we don't work as many hours.'

'I don't understand.'

'There's been lots of changes since you left. He's hired more staff, given us more flexibility. Some of us are even working from home now. Everyone leaves at five. Oh, well, if they want to. We have some big accounts to work on and everyone is pretty pumped, especially about the new recycling ones.'

'Recycling?'

'Yep, Oracle is going to be getting a lot of the government work now.'

Lucy's head spun as Tara kept talking. 'But Marcus is insisting that no one works too many hours. That's why we have so many new staff. Are you sure you don't want to come back?'

'Oh, no.' She wasn't about to tell Tara that the reason she left—the real reason—wasn't Oracle's employment conditions but the man himself.

Though, somehow Lucy guessed that Tara knew.

'He's at home. You could always find him there.' Tara winked at Lucy and her cheeks burnt.

'No, he's not.'

The voice behind her reverberated through her chest and made every pore in her body quiver.

Tara's head swivelled. 'Marcus. What are you doing here?'

'I just came to get my other laptop—I thought I might work from home tomorrow.'

His gaze moved from Tara to Lucy and now she really did wish she had thought of an explanation for her impromptu arrival.

'Hi,' he said, so softly, and her insides began to unravel. He looked different since she'd last seen him, though it had only been six weeks. The circles under his eyes more pronounced, the weight on his shoulders heavier somehow.

'Hi,' she replied, her voice breathless and barely more than a whisper.

He smiled and she wanted to sob. Marcus's smile was enough to break the resolve of the proudest woman. *Take me back, I don't need commitment. I just need you.* She closed her eyes. She should just leave.

'Lucy just dropped by to see if you have five minutes,' Tara prompted once it was apparent Lucy and Marcus had exhausted their conversation.

'In that case, would you like to come through?' He motioned to the corridor to his office.

She kept her head down as she followed him, not wanting to be recognised and not wanting to see the looks on everyone's faces. But her face was still burning by the time they reached his office and he closed the door behind them.

She wanted to reach for it and flee. Why had she come here? There was no point; she was only torturing herself more. All this impromptu visit had proven was that she was as much in love with Marcus Hawke as ever. Her limbs felt scattered, her heart wild.

'Sorry to arrive unannounced. I got your message,' she explained.

'What did you think?' He stepped back from the doorway and motioned for her to follow him to the middle of the office. She hesitated. It was strange to be back here. The room smelt of Marcus and reminded her of before and was liable to make her forget why she'd even come. And why, perhaps, it wasn't a good idea.

'I…was surprised.'

'Good surprised, bad surprised?'

'Good.' Her tone was uncertain and his brow creased.

'It wasn't what we initially designed,' he said.

'No, but I like it. I think it was great. I'm glad they went with it.'

'Me too. I don't know how I would have come

up with an excuse to get in touch with you otherwise.'

Now it was Lucy's brow's turn to furrow. 'What?'

'I wanted you to see it. I wanted you to know.'

Lucy pressed her lips together. She had no idea what he was trying to say.

'Know what?'

'That I've been using work as a crutch. As an excuse to avoid other things.'

'But that's okay.'

'No, not really. It isn't when it means I'd be missing out on the best thing that ever happened to me.'

The floor felt unsteady under her feet. Did he mean…?

'I've thought a lot about what you said, but I've also been thinking a lot about Joel. And my dad. And do you know what I think he'd have to say. About you?'

'What?' Dread gripped her. *Irresponsible, stupid*…that's what people usually said about her.

'He'd say I was a bloody idiot. To have a chance of happiness, to have a family of my own and to give it up because I was too scared or too ambitious or too something… My father would have done anything to have his family back. I was being scared. And stupid.'

'No, no, you weren't. Your goals are noble, important.'

Marcus smiled again, stepped closer and took her hand in his. Warmth spread through her, entwined with hope.

'I can still do important work. Do you know what you taught me, Lucy Spencer?'

She shook her head. It was remarkable to think that she could have taught Marcus anything.

'That having a life makes you a better employee, a better person, a better designer, a better creator. I was so focused on my job... I forgot how to look at the world, how to see it, appreciate it. In Fiji with you, I came alive. And not just because of you—though that had a lot to do with it—because for once I was actually living life.'

'I'm not sure I understand.'

'We've hired more staff, and everyone is working fewer hours.'

Lucy nodded.

'And we're happier, performing better than ever.'

'What about your dream? The big campaigns? Road safety?'

'That's the thing—we've been asked to do a series of ads on recycling. There's also talk about the next antismoking campaign.'

'Really? That's fantastic.'

He nodded, swallowed as though he were suddenly shy. 'What am I protecting, if not the people I love? Besides, do you know you work much better if you're rested? Your staff do too.'

Lucy laughed. 'You're just figuring that out?' Lucy's face was hot. What was he saying? What was he trying to say? She looked down, saw his long fingers knotted with hers.

'I was a bit slow.'

He lifted his hand and brushed a stray hair from her eyes and gently lifted her face to look at him. 'I was also too slow to tell you that I love you.'

The air left Lucy's body and the room really was spinning. Luckily, the next thing she knew Marcus was pulling her into his arms and she was the strongest person in the world. And the happiest.

EPILOGUE

THE SATURDAY WAS a double moving day.

Veronica Hawke was moving to Marcus's apartment in Woolloomooloo, and Marcus, Lucy and Lachie were moving into her townhouse in North Sydney.

One day he would buy them a bigger place, a house, but for now, this arrangement suited them perfectly. His mother's townhouse was a short walk from Lachie's school and Veronica was delighted to move to Marcus's wharf-side apartment in the bustling harbour suburb.

'Are you sure this is all right, Veronica?' Lucy asked his mother for the tenth time.

Veronica laughed. 'You're kidding, right? I'm the one getting the harbour-side apartment.' Not to mention the daughter-in-law and step-grand-child, Marcus thought. But he didn't say aloud what his mother had said when she had first suggested the house swap. His mother had not been this happy in years. Content, yes, but over the past few months Veronica Hawke had been beaming and bouncing with additional energy. She was besotted with Lachie, as Marcus had predicted, looking across now to Lachie, who was unwrapping a box of LEGO Veronica had bought him. Lachie was going to be one very spoilt boy. At least until another grandchild came along to share the bounty, which Marcus hoped would not be long.

He was the one in the hurry; Lucy was the one who wanted to wait until she had a few years' professional experience under her belt.

She was still working at Birdseye Design. He understood why it was important to her to forge her career on her own and not in his shadow. To win work on her own merits, and not because of who her partner was.

With Henry's encouragement, Lucy was learning from Henry how to run his business and he very much wanted her to take it over when he retired in the next few years. The thought of running her own business was daunting, but she knew this was one way to make sure that she could be around for Lachie, and any other children that might arrive. Marcus was as driven as ever, but had far more balance in his life. Now he had Lucy and Lachie to go home to, it was easy to step back from work. Marcus and Lachie were becoming closer and he was overjoyed to now have the chance to strengthen their relationship even further.

With Lucy's agreement he even had a special surprise planned for Lachie later that day, a puppy for their new family.

'I will buy us a house, you know.'

Lucy laughed. 'One step at a time. I'm not sure

I could handle house purchasing along with planning a wedding.' She looked down at her left hand at the simple solitary on her ring finger and shook her head. 'I'm still getting my head around this.'

The truck with Veronica's belongings departed just as the one from Marcus's apartment arrived. Veronica kissed the three of them before getting into her car. 'Enjoy this day, and this time. I love you all and am overjoyed for you.'

Lucy slipped her arm around his waist and waved her off. 'I don't know where to begin.' She sighed as she looked at the new truck and her parents' car approaching with some of her belongings.

'You don't have to do it all on your own, you know. We're a team now.'

'I know.'

'Everyone here wants to help you. They want to support us.'

The number of good wishes they had received since their engagement had been overwhelming. The staff at Oracle thought it was a fantastic development; they could feel firsthand what effect Lucy had had on Marcus. Even Lachie's father, Alex, had managed to mumble his congratulations to the pair.

'I guess I never thought I'd be this happy. I didn't think I deserved it.'

'But you know now that you do? That's there's nothing I wouldn't do for you?'

'I'm starting to realise that.'

'I swear I will spend the rest of my life proving it to you.'

He lowered his head and met her lips with his.

* * * * *

If you enjoyed this story,
check out this other great read
from Justine Lewis

Billionaire's Snowbound Marriage Reunion

Available now!